In Plain Sight

Thanks for taking an
interest in my little
project!
Dan K

a collection by

Dan Kennard

ISBN-13: 9798614353322

Cover art by Dan Kennard
Library of Congress Control Number: 2018675309
Printed in the United States of America

ACKNOWLEDGEMENTS

An earlier version of "Ouroboros" was previously published in *Jersey Devil Press* (September 2012)

An earlier version of "Pinholes" was previously published in the *Tahoma Literary Review* (December 2014)

"Foreplay" was previously published in *The Offbeat* (Spring 2015)

"Kennardo Goes to the Hospital," "Kennardo Goes Driving," and "Kennardo Goes Out for a Drink" were previously published together in *Word Riot* (May 2015)

An earlier version of "Hide and Seek" was published as "Sweet Relief" in *Weirderary* (October 2016)

"Kennardo's Balloons" was previously published in *Five:2:One* (March 2017)

"Playing with Myself" was previously published in *Straylight Literary Magazine* (March 2018)

IN PLAIN SIGHT

BY DAN KENNARD

dedicated to Stevee
for her love and support

♥

"God also likes to play hide-and-seek, but because there is nothing outside God, he has no one but himself to play with....He pretends that he is you and I and all the people in the world, all the animals, all the plants, all the rocks and all the stars. In this way he has strange and wonderful adventures, some of which are terrible and frightening. But these are just like bad dreams, for when he wakes up they will disappear."

--Alan Watts
The Book: On the Taboo Against Knowing Who You Are

TABLE OF CONTENTS

Kennardo Goes to Work

I remember it was morning, and I was walking to work. There were clouds gathering on the horizon and I was standing at a street corner eating a candy bar for breakfast, anxious for the signal to change because I was somehow late again. It was like living out a bad dream because I had already been warned that if I were late to work one more time I would be fired on the spot. I checked my phone to see how many minutes I had left before I would have to consider running through traffic to save my life, my livelihood, or end up living on the streets begging for food. Not many, it turned out.

I slid my phone back into my pocket again and when I looked up he was standing right next to me, pushing buttons on his own plastic phone that clearly wasn't a real phone, but more like a dog toy, with big colorful buttons on the front, like something that would squeak when you squeezed it, and he was pantomiming my frustration, mocking me, tapping one of his long red shoes in the same rhythm I happened to be tapping my own worn out dress shoes as we all stood waiting for the light to change. I felt myself glare at him a bit, un-amused at his act, and then I turned to toss my candy bar wrapper into the nearby trashcan like I did every morning, but for the first time I can ever remember, I missed it, a sudden gust of wind swatting the wrapper away like an invisible hand, sending it out into the street where the cars were all rushing past.

Foreplay

I started out thinking I would just sit him down at a café somewhere and have the waiter slip him a note that said "Hey Dan, guess what? You're a character in a story, your life is not a real life the way you think it is, and everything you do and everything you say and everyone you meet from now on are a fabrication of my mind. You are nothing more than a collection of my sentences!" and then sign my name at the bottom. But when I sat down to write the scene I realized I couldn't go through with it. Not only did it feel too harsh, just to put all of that on him out of the blue, but it also turned out to be much more complicated than that. Besides, I can't ignore the fact that if he is some kind of distorted reflection of myself, a character made in my own image, then he probably wouldn't believe a note like that anyway, so I decided to take it slow and try to prove it to him scene-by-scene.

The first thing I did was give him a new girlfriend named Kenndra and set them up on a date. Let's just say that they met at their community center art class, and he loved the way her shoulder-length blonde hair was always falling over her eyes, creating the impression that she was always half-turned away from him or half in shadow, hard to make eye contact with. By the end of the four-week class he had earned her phone number, and a few days later he called to ask her out.

Now, in the dim yellow light of a restaurant, he looked at her over their half-finished food and drinks, admiring how delicate and feminine her fingers were compared to his as she held the stem of her wine glass and looked around the restaurant, and it was right in the middle of that thought when I decided to call him.

"Excuse me," he said, putting his fork down and pulling his phone out.

I made him make a funny face and then made Kenndra say, "Is everything all right?"

"It was just a bunch of zeros," he said, slipping it back into his pocket.

"A bunch of zeros?"

"Yeah. You ever see that?" he asked, picking up his fork again.

"Never."

"Must be some corporate thing. Probably got my number off a list somewhere." He forked some French fries into his mouth and chewed.

"What list?"

"Lists, you know? Like businesses get information from lists."

"I didn't know that. Where do the lists come from?" She was being sarcastic.

"Internet databases. Of course all these places have

secret deals with the government or whatever too." He swiped his beard with a folded napkin. "You know what I mean."

"Do I?"

"Listen, that's not even the point. We're getting bogged down in details now. Here's my point, when these places call, they hide the number like that so people like you will be more likely to answer. Not me though."

"People like me? What does that mean?"

"You know what I mean."

"I really don't think I do, but your unbridled certainty about the whole process is very compelling."

"I'm trying to demonstrate confidence so that you'll fall in love with me."

She looked skeptically over the table at him, but Dan was delighted, imagining he had finally met the perfect girl, a girl who he can really banter with, and he was so glad that he decided to join that art workshop. He almost didn't, and he hadn't painted anything since it ended, but it was the summer and he didn't feel like watching television and drinking beer at home every night. He grinned across the table at her, thinking for a moment that this was all too good to be true. The trouble for me was finding the best way to tell him he was right. I had to get his attention somehow.

I realized that if I wanted him to know he wasn't real—that nothing was real at all—I would have to get in his face a little more and really make my presence felt, so after the date while he was driving Kenndra home I decided to call him again even though I knew he wouldn't answer. At this stage, I felt like the best thing I could do was to be disruptive.

It started ringing, and she looked down at his pocket, the phone glowing through his khakis. It continued to ring as he worked it from his pants, and when he pulled it out he saw the zeros on the screen again.

"Same number?" said Kenndra.

"Yeah." He looked at the screen, feeling it vibrate in his hand while he waited for it to go to voicemail.

"So you're not going to answer it?" She looked at him from the passenger seat and tucked a strand of hair behind her ear.

"I don't like to answer calls from numbers I don't know." He clicked the screen dark, and pushed it back into his pocket again.

"I think you should answer it next time. I mean really," said Kenndra, "what's the worst that could happen?"

"The revelation of an unsettling truth?" I made him say.

"But you won't know anything until you answer it."

"I'm at peace with not knowing anything. My life is good precisely because there are certain things I don't know."

"That bothers me," she said. "Something about that bothers me."

I made him wait to call her again for another date, so here we all are three days later and if he was being honest with himself, he was a little nervous on the phone. Who wouldn't be? He liked Kenndra. In fact, it was safe to say he was falling in love with her. He loved her lithe fingers and her blonde hair, and the way they could talk with ease, but like me he knew he had to take it slow, he had to pace himself so he could get it right.

"So what do you think?" he said. "Dinner and a movie?" He was in his kitchen pacing back-and-forth in his underwear, looking down at his socked feet and touching his crotch absently.

"Sure. What movie?"

"I'll see whatever. I just want to hold your hand and

squeeze your thigh in the dark."

"Well that will depend on which movie you pick," she said.

"Are those the rules?"

"Those are the rules."

"I'll surprise you then. I'll try to imagine myself as you and decide that way. I'll ask myself: What movie would give me the best chance to squeeze Kenndra's thigh?"

There was silence for a moment, and all of a sudden his heart ached at the idea that he was being too forward or that she didn't feel the same way he did. He thought for a flitting second that Kenndra was becoming weary of him, or that maybe he was showing too much of his own weirdness, but really it was my fault. For a second I had thought of taking Kenndra away from him.

"Kenndra?"

"Yeah?"

"I thought we got disconnected."

"No, I'm still here."

"So what do you think?"

"Pick me up at five-thirty," she said.

This time I decided he would take her to the Quack House, a fine French restaurant in downtown Sunset City known for its roast duck, so between that, and the names, and all the loaded dialogue, I was really starting to pile it on.

I decided to write myself in for a moment, so now I am waiting and watching from a corner booth, brushing the lapels of my tattered brown suit as I watch him lift his first beer from the table and move it towards his mouth, watching and waiting until I see his lips barely touch the white foam, and it's at that precise moment that I call him again. Feeling my phone ring in his pocket caused him to put the beer down after a short little half-sip and take his phone out. Back at their table he looks at the screen and says,

"It's the zeros."

"You still haven't answered?"

"I told you my rule about phone numbers."

"What if it's important?"

"Then they would leave a message and I would call them back. That's actually the first one I've gotten since the last time I saw you."

"Really?"

"Yeah," he said, both of them pausing, feeling the bone-deep sensation of what it's like to live through space breaks, no real memory of anything but each other, no experiences except the ones I give them.

"That's weird, right? That makes me nervous all of a sudden."

They didn't notice me looking straight at them from the corner booth, holding my overs-sized phone against my ear.

"It's just a phone call," he said to Kenndra.

"You don't know what it is until you answer it. It's driving me crazy that you haven't answered it yet. And why do they only call when I'm around?"

"I don't know," he said, tucking the phone back into his pants pocket. "How would I know?"

"Well it makes me nervous. It doesn't make you nervous? Is someone, like, following us or something? You know what I mean? The more I think about it, the more I'm like, what the fucks with the calls?"

"I'll answer it next time," he said. "And I don't think anyone is following us. Who would follow us?"

"Can you call them back?"

"Right now?"

"Please?"

"Really? You're really worked up about this? It's just a phone call."

"A lot of things start with just a phone call. It would make me feel better to just find out who they are and what they want," she said. "I feel involved now. I'm as much a part of this as you are."

"How about I call them back after dinner? I want to enjoy our date first."

"Me too…so could you please call them back right now?"

"After dinner. I promise."

Next thing they knew dinner was over and they were back in his car again. Dan was returning my call while Kenndra sat sideways in the passenger seat, staring at him with an anxious look on her face. After a few seconds, he turned to her with the phone to his ear and said, "It just keeps ringing."

"Is there voicemail?"

"Not yet."

Outside, the parking lot lights glowed dim orange, casting their faces in dappled shadow as they looked at each other inside the car, sitting together in the darkness and silence of the near-empty parking lot deep within the dimly lit room I'm writing all this from, but down in the car I made sure they could both hear it ringing.

"I'm hanging up," I made him say. "No one is answering."

At my computer, I was biting my lip, typing and deleting, typing and deleting, second-guessing what I had planned to say, but reminding myself that I should probably keep it short. Despite my impatience I kept returning to the idea that I didn't have to throw back the curtains all at once, that there would always be more stories to put them through. I reminded myself that this was only the beginning, that this was just foreplay.

He dropped his phone into an empty cup holder between them and turned on the car, but before he could even strap on his seat belt, I called him back. I was ready. I knew what I was going to say.

Kenndra turned to face him and said, "It's the zeros, isn't it. They're calling us back." They both looked down at his phone, the screen glowing with a string of zeros. Now that I was ready they were ready too, and they looked each other straight in the eyes for what felt like the first time, before he finally touched the screen and put the phone to his ear.

Kennardo Goes to the Hospital

His first and only recorded appearance came when he showed up on the security cameras of the Sunset City Children's Hospital tramping through the hallways in the really early morning in that tattered brown suit of his with his white face and brown half-crushed hat on his head, visiting the sick children.

He would stand at their bedside, watching them sleep and clutching his hands together over his heart in pantomimed anguish as if he knew we were watching him on the cameras, drawing attention to himself with his exaggeration, outwardly projecting his sympathy for their plight, and after clutching his hands together over his heart he would kiss the tips of his fingers and press them to their foreheads tenderly, making a real show of it, making it ceremonial almost. I remember that before he would leave their bedsides, he would reach into his jacket pocket and take out a piece of candy or a package of crayons like you would get for your kids at a restaurant, or even sometimes a vase with a single yellow daisy in it, and he would leave them on the bedside table for when they woke up. As we watched him pass from one screen to the next on our security monitors, mesmerized, I remember my partner saying, "Is he trying to be funny? Or is he just being sarcastic?"

"I don't know," I replied, crossing my arms and studying the screen intently, like he was a puzzle. "Where did the doctors and nurses go?"

My partner moved his face closer to the screen and said, "That's a great question. It's like they've gone poof."

"What is this? What's going on?" I said.

Neither of us knew what to think, but as we would soon discover, the most curious element about it all—other than the sudden sight of a hobo-clown on hospital security cameras—is that there was no footage of him actually entering or exiting the building. It was as if he appeared out of thin air, like he was some kind of trickster that was able to move between borders in space and time, an inter-galactic jokester of some sort. By the time we sent someone down to confront him, he was already gone again, vanishing like darkness from a lighted room.

Kennardo Goes Grocery Shopping

I didn't know it was legal to buy as much beer at one time as he did, cases and cases of it, virtually emptying the entire domestic beer section to the point where he needed the assistance of the whole grocery store staff. After we had all worked together to form a train of several shopping carts and weaved our way towards the front register, each cart stacked chest-high with cases of beer, as I began checking him out I said, "So where's the party?"

He looked at me aloof and said, "What party?"

"I mean what's the occasion? Why are you buying all of this beer?"

Without answering me, he began looking for his wallet, reaching deep into his coat pockets, then patting at his chest, then patting at the baggy legs of his pants, pulling his jacket pockets inside-out and sending bits of colored construction paper and glitter fluttering to the ground.

"There's no occasion," he said finally, searching the

inside pockets of his jacket, which upon inspection seemed to be filled with candy wrappers and paper clips that he dropped into one or another of his hands, then, when seeing they weren't his wallet, dropped it all back into his pockets again. "The beer is for me," he announced. "I'm stocking up for the apocalypse."

I didn't know what to say to that. I hadn't heard about any apocalypse, but I don't read the news much either. Honestly, I wasn't totally sure what an apocalypse even was. Then suddenly he snapped his fingers in delight, and lifted one of his over-sized clown shoes up from the floor and plucked a brown wallet from the sole of his shoe where it had apparently been misplaced the whole time.

He paid for all of his beer with a card and then a bunch of us helped him wheel it all out to his car, following him through the parking lot towards a rusted-out piece-of-shit sedan with a smashed-in taillight, and which we all recognized immediately would not have the space to contain all of the beer that he bought.

"Is this some kind of a joke or what? What is this?" I said as we came to a stop near his trunk. Our little crew stood there staring between the beer and his car with our hands on our hips, glancing at each other, no doubt thinking about how we were going to have to refund this asshole and restock most of the beer again, and I got the sense that he was intentionally wasting our time. I remember thinking that maybe he wasn't the funny kind of clown.

"It'll fit," he said. "This is a big trunk."

He went over to it and lifted it open, releasing hundreds of red balloons upward into the sky, a red trail of them pouring forth from the darkness of his trunk and soon enough extending into the gray clouds that hung over everything.

Turns out he wasn't joking.

Pinholes

I start by imagining that I have poked a thousand tiny holes in the lid of an imaginary shoebox and placed them inside where they will experience whatever I decide they will experience. Right now they are both lying on their backs with their hands behind their heads, their feet crossed at the ankles, their white socks showing between pant and shoe, and they are both staring, staring, staring at the roof of my shoebox, eyes serene. After a while Kenndra says, "Dan? Do you ever wonder what's beyond the stars?"

Now that I have made her ask the question, I have given myself the task of formulating a response. I immediately give him the appearance of someone thinking: the furrowing brow of a man trying to articulate complicated thoughts to himself, a sudden strain flashing in his eyes. He appears to think another moment, naturally unable to speak until I give him the words to start talking. I decide to make him clear his throat in a way that announces he might start to speak any second, but really I am deciding for myself what to make him say next. Kenndra rolls her head towards him waiting for an answer expectantly, but I am the one who is under pressure because this is all about me.

I think about telling them the truth: that they aren't stars at all, that they are pinholes, and that they are characters in my short stories, and for this one I have decided to set their story inside a closed shoebox. I want to tell them that the utter darkness around them is something like the edge of creation, and that even the words they appear to speak are the fabrications of my mind. I want them to realize they will only ever have existence when the sentences of which they are composed are read and imagined within someone else's distant mind, but then I stop and think a minute. I question my motives. I put myself in their position, which doesn't seem that hard to do. I ask myself if I would want to know the things I want them to know if I were in the same position, which in so many ways I am, and so it's easy to see why I'm hesitating with his response to her. I need to take a breath and think about it, and in the end, I decide to grant him a dim awareness.

"Beyond the stars is the man who controls everything," he says, referring to me.

I am the man beyond the stars.

Outside the box, I start whistling a tune.

"Hear that?" says Dan. They are standing next to each other in the center of the empty-shoebox-darkness that is all they know. He points at the top of the shoebox, up at the pinholes that they think are stars.

"What is it?" says Kenndra.

"It's the man beyond the stars, and he's whistling. Do you hear it?"

"I hear it. Is it good that he's whistling?"

"I think it's amazing to know that he's real, that he's really out there."

"But does he care for us?" she asks.

"I think so. I think he does."

"But how do you know? How will you ever know?"

He looks from the pinholes to Kenndra and the figure that is me stops whistling.

"Did he stop?" she asks, and for a few long seconds everything is silent.

Outside the box, I wiggle my flashlight to make it seem like the pinhole-stars are twinkling.

Later on, they are standing in the middle of the shoebox holding burning candles for light, and there is a mailbox between them.

"Hey," says Dan. "I wonder if we got any mail today?"

Kenndra opens the mailbox and reaches inside, where I have left them an envelope. She pulls it out and shows it to Dan. "Here," she says, handing it to him.

He looks from the envelope to Kenndra and says, "Are you sure you don't want to open it?" and offers to hand it back to her. She shrugs. "Suit yourself," he says, slipping a finger under the seal and ripping it open. He pulls out the piece of yellow notebook paper I put in there and begins to unfold it. They lean in closer with their candles.

"What does it say?"

I make him clear his throat again. "It says, 'Be careful with those candles because you live inside a shoebox.'"

"Is that it?"

"That's it. At the bottom it's signed, 'Yours Truly, Dan Kennard.'"

"Who is Dan Kennard?"

They stand silent in the flame-enhanced darkness,

candles burning.

"He must be the man beyond the stars. Who else could he be?"

"Do you think we really live inside a shoebox?" she asks.

"I don't know, but if we do, he's right—we should blow out these candles," and without another word he blows them out and they are swallowed up by the darkness again. A few seconds later, I take a knife and slash a short line through the top of the shoebox to simulate a shooting star.

I've decided they will carry their knowledge with them through the space breaks, so the thought that they live inside a shoebox is still present within their minds, despite everything else changing around them. So what initially appeared to be a shooting star when I first slashed through the top of the box is now just a short and permanent line in their sky, and it doesn't take long before Kenndra begins to start putting two-and-two together.

"Dan, if we live in a shoebox, then those aren't real stars, right?"

They are sitting next to each other in lawn chairs now while behind them a gas lantern burns from a picnic table with an audible hiss, casting a perfect circle of light around them as they eat their peanut butter and jelly sandwiches and stare up at the lid of the shoebox, their shadows stretching off into the darkness in front of them.

"What do you think they are then?"

"I think that if we really live in a shoebox, then they're probably just...pinholes."

"But they look like stars, right? We've seen them twinkle." He looks over at her and sucks a bit of peanut butter from the tip of his index finger.

"I've been thinking too…if we live in a shoebox, where did we get these sandwiches?" She holds her half-eaten sandwich up in the hissing light.

"I suppose they were given to us by the man outside the box."

"When?"

"I don't remember," he says, chewing. "Do you?"

"No. But I remember there was a mailbox and a letter before—and candles. Now we're sitting in lawn chairs eating sandwiches. What happened to the other stuff?"

"I haven't thought about it too much," he says. "I'm so focused on this sandwich."

"I don't think I want to live in a shoebox anymore." She stands from her lawn chair and walks over to the table with the lantern, and then she gets the sudden urge to try and escape.

"What are you doing over there?" says Dan, twisting around in his chair, watching her with a look of concern, his face cast in half-shadow.

"I'm taking this lantern and leaving," she says, picking up the lantern from the table. "I'm going to get out of here."

She looks at Dan with defiance, then wades off into the darkness of the shoebox beyond, straight into the edge of creation, holding the lantern out in front of her, and just as Dan begins to fade out of sight behind her, I end the story, along with all her hopes of escape.

Kennardo Goes to the Coffee Shop

The coffee shop was experiencing a mid-morning rush for coffees and cappuccinos, and as my mind drifted toward the work I was doing, the noise of his typing just became one more sound in the air, no better or worse than any of the other sounds we were making: the gurgling of coffee being made, the hissing cappuccinos being foamed, the occasional burst of laughter from the two women by the window who meet every day at the same time, the mechanical zings and woops of my cash register opening and closing, the general chatter of customers talking, the clinking of cups and silverware, and on and on, and you get the picture.

While I was too preoccupied with my work to notice him at first, it became apparent soon enough that he had very quickly become something of an attraction for everyone else. People entering the shop began to stop next to his table and stare at him as if he were an exhibit before moving on to their own table or coming up to the counter to order, seemingly mesmerized by him for a few moments, induced perhaps by the complete shock of his presence there looking the way he did, with his tattered brown suit and old hat, the flaky white paint on his face and his blood red puffball nose. And it was also obvious as soon as you paid any attention to him that due to the way he was typing—wild, almost slapping at the keys—that there was no way what he was typing could ever make any sense. From my point of view, it was the writing equivalent of someone bashing at a piano. I turned to Dan, who was foaming a cappuccino a few feet away and said, "Who brings a typewriter to a coffee shop anyway?"

Dan shrugged. "Did you know some people still write whole novels by hand?" He raised the metal cup of milk higher on the machine, which increased the steaming and hissing sounds as he waited for it to reach the perfect temperature. He looked at me and said, "What do you think? Should we ask him to stop?"

Dan was always asking me questions like that, like he was testing me to see what I'd say and sometimes I thought he was flirting with me because of the way he said it, kind of grinning weird. "I don't know," I finally said. "I guess not."

At the register, a lady handed me her money and said, "What's up with the clown at the typewriter? Is he allowed to be dressed like that in here? Like a tramp?"

"I'm not sure, ma'am. You'll have to discuss that with the manager."

"He makes me uncomfortable," she said. "I can't be the only one."

I smiled without responding and handed her back her change, then she walked away to wait for her drink at the other end of the counter. I looked around for Dan and found him pouring ground coffee into the slow-drip coffee machine behind me, and decided to ask him what the lady at the counter had just asked me. As he listened, he crumbled the empty paper bag in his hands and tossed it into the trash under the counter, and then turned to me serious looking.

"Like, by law?" He wiped his hands on the belly of his apron, uncertain of himself.

"I don't know. I told the lady at the end of the counter that I would speak to the manager about it, and you're pretty much the manager, right?"

"Right."

"Because I know I'm not the manager, and we're the only two people working right now."

"Yes. Exactly."

"So you're agreeing to that? You're the manager?"

"It's logical based on the context."

"By the way, she's waiting for her latte."

"Why aren't you making it?"

"You never taught me, Dan. I only ever work the register." He began rinsing the metal mug at the tiny sink we had next to the row of coffee machines. I waited for him to turn the water off before I said, "Do you think he's an actor? I think he's just acting."

He faced me again with the same look of uncertainty; his head cocked slightly, wheels turning behind his eyes. I got him good with that one, stunned him.

"Acting? That's interesting. I like that."

The lady came back to the register where the two of us were standing and said, "Excuse me, but I've been waiting on my latte for a few minutes. Is anyone making it yet?"

"We were discussing the clown," said Dan.

"I asked him what you asked me," I explained. "He's pretty much the manager."

"Well? What are you going to do about him? I don't think he's allowed to be here like that," she said. "He's scares me. There's something about him that scares me."

"I wouldn't say he's scary. I'm not scared of him," said Dan.

"Potentially threatening maybe?" I offered.

"Threatening, yes," agreed the lady. She seemed insistent, and then I had the flashing thought that she was only there to push us towards the climax, like we were all suddenly actors in a scene and her role was to nudge us onwards.

"Do you think he's acting?" I asked the lady, curious to hear her answer.

"I don't know what he's doing, but somebody needs to find out. And somebody else needs to make my latte, I have to get out of here, I'm late."

"Are you going to talk to him?" I said to Dan.

"No, you are."

"Not me," I said. "Too weird."

"But you don't know how to make a latte," said Dan, pouncing on me.

"You never taught me! Really, Dan? You're the manager. You just agreed to that like five seconds ago. Confronting customers is a manager thing."

"So then, as manager, due to your ignorance of lattes, I am forced to abdicate my responsibilities to you so that I may do what you cannot."

"You're so lame."

"Thank you," he said, making his weird grin again.

"So what should I say to him?"

"He hasn't bought anything yet, right? So tell him if he doesn't buy anything soon he's going to have to leave. There's your story. Do I have to do all the work around here?"

I took a deep breath before I walked over to the clown man, and as I approached him I decided to be straight up with him. "Sir, are you an actor? We want to know what you're doing. What is this?" He looked up at me annoyed, like I was interrupting him, his typing stopping for the first time in almost half an hour or more. He didn't say anything at first, just sat silent, breathing heavily from the manner in which he had been typing for so long. "Why are you writing on a typewriter? It's kind of clunky to be carrying around, isn't it? You don't have a laptop?"

"I do not," he said indignantly. "And if you have no other business, I ask that you please leave me alone, I'm right in the middle of a scene at the moment. One of my characters is trying to hook up his cable, and I'm really giving him the run-around."

My confrontation with him had become the center of everyone's attention at that point. Some people were clearly amused, while others, like the latte lady, felt threatened and uncomfortable. I didn't know how to feel, personally, but I also had a job to do. I put my hands on my hips authoritatively and said, "If you aren't going to buy anything soon then we might have to ask you to leave."

He tipped his head back and let out a long sigh. "Do we have to do this right now? Right in the middle of this scene?"

"I'm sorry, sir, but we've been building up to this. You've been here a little while already and you haven't actually bought anything yet, which is a problem for us on a policy level, and which is why we thought maybe you were an actor."

"All I have is a fistful of rubber bands," he said, lifting a handful out of his jacket pocket and dropping them on the edge of the table, a multi-colored nest of circles. "How many rubber bands for a hot black coffee?"

"You're joking, right?"

"About which part?"

I turned around to look at Dan for backup, but he was just finishing up the latte, handing it to the woman at the end of the counter.

"You're scaring some of the other customers," I said.

The lady realized we were talking about her and stopped next to me to confront him herself as she passed by us. "I don't like you," she said, pointing a finger at him. "There's something wrong about you, and we all know it."

He made an over-exaggerated frowny face, which only served to further annoy the woman and next thing I knew another customer piped in and said, "Calm down, lady, he's allowed to be here," so then the latte lady turned to that person and said, "Who the hell are you to tell me to calm down!" and then Dan came walking over and stepped between them saying, "Everybody needs to calm down or I'll be calling the police," positioning himself between them like a boxing referee, and then someone else stood up and said, "You should call them anyway to have that man arrested!" and then the entire coffee shop sprung into an uproar of debate.

Every single customer in the diner was on one side or another, everyone had their own interpretations of him, and people were standing out of their chairs and shouting at each other in a frenzy, until a minute later in walked two police officers, wondering what's going on, holding up their badges and batons, trying to establish order from the chaos, but when it was all explained to them they each took opposing sides too like everyone else, in heated debate with each other as to how the law applied in this particular case, and it went on and on like that until more officers arrived to really break it all up on the grounds of a "public disturbance." Then the debate as to who had actually created the disturbance in the first place became its own issue, and it became a real mess after that.

Anyway, sometime during the whole thing, we all took our eyes off of him, and just like no one could recall seeing him come in, once we realized he was gone, no one could recall seeing him leave either. His typewriter was gone along with him, and the only thing left behind as proof he was really there was the pile of multi-colored rubberbands he had offered as payment, which we eventually ended up throwing in the trash.

What else were we supposed to do with them?

Hot Black Coffee

Ever since I took my seat at the very back of the plane, all I could think about was how badly I wanted a cup of hot black coffee, as if I was born desiring it, so when we finally achieved altitude and the flight attendant emerged way up at the front of the aisle behind her cart, almost blurry through the great distance between us, it felt like waiting for destiny to approach me one row at a time. Luckily I had brought a book to distract my mind a bit as I waited because I knew mine would be the longest wait of anyone on the plane, situated as I was in the very last seat of the very last row.

I was cheery enough at first anticipating the moment that I would be able to hold the hot cup of coffee between my hands, so much so that I was able to imagine it there on my tiny tray table, right next to my open book, steaming and dark, looking at my reflection in its glassy surface. You could say that in many ways it was the idea of the hot black coffee in my mind that excited me more than anything else because I was fully aware that it might end up not being a very good cup of coffee. It could be some cheap, watery kind with barely a taste to it or they might only have French Vanilla or Hazelnut left by the time they got to me, which would be a certain kind of travesty. Can you imagine waiting for something so long and then getting it, only to realize it either isn't very good in the first place or that perhaps you no longer even want it at all? Haha! Or, imagine waiting so long only to discover that because I was last in line they have run out of the coffee I still very much desired—the horror of that pronouncement!—it being the thing that I still very much viewed as a symbol of my personal destiny to attain, and imagine further my dogged insistence that they brew another pot, just for me, which in itself would only add more time to my wait to the point that maybe they either wouldn't have enough time to make it before landing, or, if they did, lead to me not having time enough to drink it. What a nightmare that would be! What a disappointing, wasted flight in the end! Haha! But alas, being aware that all of those scenarios were mere speculation and that reality was unfolding right in front of me, I managed to stifle my fancies by telling myself that I would have to be patient regardless and there was no use torturing myself by thinking about it too much.

I read my book in an effort to pass the time, and like many people reading on planes, between short bouts of reading I found myself wanting to gaze out of a window contemplatively in order to think about what I had just read and admire the blue world outside, but there was a problem: it turned out that I was so far in the back of the plane that I had no access to a window at all! Haha! What a break, what luck, to have instead only a window-shaped depression in the plastic wall where there should have been a window. It seemed as if someone had once had the vague idea to one day place a window there, but for whatever reason had decided not to, a fact that I will admit depressed me slightly and which somehow felt directed at me personally. Nonetheless, I straightened myself up in my seat, regained my poise a bit, and told myself it was no matter, that I didn't need a window like everyone else because I didn't need the same things everyone else needed because I had the conviction deep-down that I was living a life closer to the bone of existence, a life without all the superficial fluff, including windows, and had therefore come to know things that no one else would ever know. I told myself that enlightenment doesn't derive from looking out plane windows or having the most legroom or being the first in line for drinks, but is rather something that can be achieved under any circumstances, and so with some of my cheer restored, I forced myself to read another page of my book.

A few minutes later (for it was a dense book, often requiring recursive rereading of whole passages in order to understand), I looked up again to check the status of the flight attendant, and I saw with dread that she had barely moved. Because I couldn't exactly remember where she was before I had resolved to continue reading, I couldn't say definitively that she hadn't moved at all, but she was still blurry enough through the distance that it couldn't have been more than a row or two. I sighed involuntarily, an exhale of breath that escaped my body like a soul upon death. I began to sense that perhaps it would be a longer wait for my coffee than I anticipated and I checked my watch to see how long we had been flying and to calculate how long it would be until we landed again. Despite the pace of things so far, I was able to convince myself that conditions would improve, that the pace of the flight attendant's progress down the aisle towards me would increase—it had to!—and that soon enough, perhaps after reading a few more pages of my book, I would have my cup of coffee in hand because, you see, in my best moments I am an optimist.

I looked towards the wall next to me, forgetting for a moment that there was no window, and chuckled at my lapse of memory before turning back to my book again. It was a good book, written long ago and full of long sentences about abstract ideas that I doubted anyone else on the plane could appreciate if they were even able to read them at all, if they were even able to make it from one end to the other like I could, a feat that had anyone ever asked me to demonstrate they would find I could accomplish with an ease and grace that would somehow prove that I, in a roundabout way, deserved a better seat on the plane than I had been randomly assigned. The way I see it, reading lengthy sentences should be a more highly-valued skill than it is in our world, especially for the people who go out of their way to read them when they could otherwise be reading such simpler, shorter ones like everyone else. Simply put, should I ever read them aloud, should a group of people gather to witness my performance, I wouldn't find it unreasonable whatsoever if those same people were compelled to throw money or roses at my feet the same way they do for other performers in the other arts. To be appreciated! To have my talent recognized! What a world! I could even imagine a world where someone, perhaps on their way to the bathroom, saw what I was reading and, knowing the kinds of sentences my book contained, offered to switch seats with me on the spot! Haha! They would recognize my book as something they had always wanted to read, but never could, and they would remark to me about how they couldn't even get past the first page upon seeing that I was well into the thick of it myself, all the while gathering my things and going about switching places with them. But of course I was fully aware that would never happen for me; I wasn't delusional.

I was, however, beginning to think that if things didn't pick up soon I would be lucky to get my hot black coffee at all the way things were going.

I stared towards the front of the plane as if the entire scene in front of me were an exhibit of sorts, watching the flight attendant work, watching her nodding vigorously and smiling politely at what were undoubtedly a series of stupid, silly questions from the people she was serving. What could they possibly have questions about? What sorts of compelling things could she be nodding at so vigorously? How was she able to keep such a professional demeanor through it all? I have many personal strengths, but I will admit that had our positions been reversed one of my weaknesses would no doubt have been exposed, which is that I have a low tolerance for the kinds of idiotic questions I imagined those people to be asking her, and that I would not have been able to maintain the polite façade so easily as she seemed to, a feat I actually came to admire as I continued to watch her work her way, slowly, towards me.

The sight of another man in an aisle seat further up (who I watched with some measure of jealousy and resentment happily receive a cup of hot black coffee from the flight attendant) caused me to think of something which I hadn't thought so much about, which was how did I end up getting the very last seat in the very last row of the plane, without a window, and with no doubt the least amount of legroom of anyone? What poor luck! How badly in that moment I wanted to switch places with that man! How badly in that moment I wanted to be someone else, have someone else's advantageous position! It caused me to think about a lot of things, none of which were helpful or productive, but which nonetheless I couldn't help but ponder.

First was the idea that this man, whoever he was, would

very likely be finished with his coffee long before I ever received mine, and the notion of unfairness in that began to drive me mad. Surely I deserved my cup of coffee as much or more than anyone else on that plane, and yet I would be the last to receive it. Haha! What a world! There was a chance, too, that should he request it, he could have a second or third cup of coffee long before I ever had my first, and on top of it all, I doubted his ability to appreciate the luxury and glamour of his own position because very few people were capable of that kind of self-reflection. I (pessimistically I will admit, this not being one of my best moments) doubted seriously how grateful that man was to already have his cup of coffee while so many others waited behind him for theirs. Did he even think about that fact of his privilege? Did he feel shame or embarrassment over it? It seemed unlikely. He got his coffee and the rest of us waiting behind him could just fuck off is what he was most likely thinking. I doubt he gave any thought at all to the fact that he wasn't me and that was precisely what made him so lucky, his position being the result of good fortune bestowed upon him long before the plane ever left the ground.

I thought pessimistically that he probably even thought he deserved his good seat; that if I were to ask him straightforwardly, he would say that he somehow earned it moreso than I, and then I got to the point where I had to tell myself to stop. I didn't know this man, and I didn't know what he felt about himself, so I had to admit I was being harsh towards him, and I tried to open myself up to the possibility that perhaps one day me and that man could even become friends, brought together by our mutual desire for hot black coffee. Perhaps after exiting the plane we will run into each other at one of the bathroom stalls in the terminal and I will remark about how good or bad I thought the coffee was on the plane and he would agree with me and we will form a fast friendship over it all. Who am I kidding though? What an admittedly creepy thing to do anyway! Besides, he might have finished his coffee so long ago by that point that he will have forgotten his opinion of it completely while my opinion would still be fresh in my head, not to mention the risk of us possibly having different opinions about it altogether. I sat back in my seat and traced the window-shaped depression with my eyes, doing everything I could, utilizing every technique of self control that I had to stop obsessing over the coffee I desired so badly, for I still desired it just as much, maybe even moreso, than I had when we had first taken off. I closed my eyes and optimistically told myself that my moment would be coming soon enough, and I spent a few moments visualizing myself receiving my own cup of coffee with a humility and grace far exceeding anyone else's despite my position at the absolute back of the plane, planning as I was to receive it from the flight attendant in such a way as to reveal the depth of my gratitude.

When I opened my eyes again from my reverie, I had reminded myself that with the proper approach to things, I could transcend my resentment and jealousy of everyone else in front of me who was already sipping their coffee and live on a higher plane of existence, no longer suffering over my lack of windows and legroom and coffee. Let them have their drinks! I thought. Enjoy them! I will have mine soon enough too, and then we will all be happy. But I went another step forward: I told myself, not only will I be happy, I will be fulfilled, I will have gained insights no one else had gained because I will have endured more than anyone else! Haha! Soon enough, I came to understand my position on the plane as something of a service to others, telling myself that should anyone else have had the misfortune of being put where I was without the tools I possessed they would surely break apart—but not me! I was put here because I was one of the few who could actually handle it and whoever was responsible for assigning everyone's seats must have known that about me. I smiled at the thought of my superiority, rationalized or not, and went back to reading my book again.

To me, there was no better way to pass the time than with a superior book full of long, abstract sentences. Most people only listened to headphones or watched movies and those who did read often only read books with short sentences, which I assumed was because of their inability to read and appreciate the kinds of long sentences I could. If only they knew what they were missing! Oh well, I guess. What can one do? While it may be true that everyone else had an advantageous position on the plane, I realized that I had an advantageous position of the mind and that fact alone should have appeased me—and for a while it did. My initial desires for a window to gaze from or legroom to stretch in or coffee to drink suddenly seemed petty in comparison to my other advantages, and so I was able to let them go for the moment. Compassion swept over me and suddenly I found myself thinking, at least temporarily, that everything had worked out perfectly in a way, and so I threw myself back into my reading again.

Some time passed—I don't know how much—but because of the nature of my reading material and my recursive approach to reading it, it wasn't long until I found my eyes growing weary and tired as they scanned the pages, and, of course, what better thing than a cup of hot black coffee to help me push through the fatigue! Haha! There I was again, thinking of the coffee, and trying desperately not to look up, not to check how much progress the flight attendant had made with her metal cart because I did not want to disappoint myself again or set my mind reeling from its current state of peace and contentment, but I couldn't help it! I raised my eyes a bit and saw that she had moved closer, but she was still far enough away from me that I couldn't help but grow frustrated. It felt like a joke was being played on me!

With my book open on my lap, I watched intensely from my seat, scrutinizing everyone through the distance, finding quite easily many areas in which the process of distributing drinks and snacks could be sped up so that I might one day enjoy my cup of hot black coffee. For one thing, too many people seemed to misunderstand what drinks were available to them, causing the stewardess to have to repeat the list several times. Even then, it's not as if anyone knew what they wanted like I did. They still had to think about it, as if it was the most important choice of their lives, and I wanted to get up out of my seat and confront them over what can only be rightly perceived as utter rudeness. I wanted to lean into their faces like the flight attendant and demand they pick something, and fast, because there were more people to serve behind them who have been waiting patiently who would also like a drink and who already know what they want— people like me!

Besides, how much of the flight was even left? Who would even want to know the time if they were in my position? I shuddered at the thought of checking, aware of the panic that would come with finding out there was hardly any time left at all while I sat there with nothing, my existence at the back of the plane unacknowledged from start to finish, my tiny tray table with only a book and no coffee. Haha! How depressing! I began to consider leaving my seat and going straight up to the cart myself, interrupting the whole scene to demand my cup of coffee on the spot before it was too late. I could picture myself doing it, I could picture myself pointing impatiently at my watch as if to say, "Can we get on with it, please? I'd like a cup of coffee like that guy up there already has," and I would point to the guy behind her with my jealousy evident upon my face and in my eyes, and I would show her my book as if it were some kind of license that entitled me to my coffee on the spot. But alas, these are mere thoughts, pure fantasy, and so all I really did was turn my book over and read the book jacket again, and then without thinking about it, involuntarily, as if my arm were no longer under my own control, I reached up and pushed my overhead button to call for a flight attendant.

She arrived immediately from somewhere behind me as if she had been waiting for me to push the call button the whole time, and then she leaned in close to speak through the incredible roar of the engines on the other side of my plastic wall.

"Yes, sir? You pushed the call button?" she shouted, barely audible through the noise.

"I would like a cup of hot black coffee please!" I shouted back.

She stood back from me with a confused, annoyed look on her face and then looked up the aisle towards the cart, willing me to look with her as if I didn't know the cart was up there, as if I hadn't been watching it since it first appeared what felt like a whole lifetime ago. Then she leaned in towards me again and said, "The only coffee we have is on the cart, sir!" pointing towards the front of the plane.

"I know that!" I shouted back. I *want* some is what I'm saying. I deserve some. Why is it taking so long? I'm in a seat without any windows, I'm sharpening my brain instead of dulling it like the rest of you," I said, implicating every other passenger in the cabin around me. I don't know what made me do it, but I felt myself rising theatrically from my seat, like a character being inflated into life, except my seatbelt was still clipped. I must have been making a bit of a scene, because everyone was suddenly looking down the aisle at me.

"Sir," she leaned in closer to me and suddenly it was if the engines were no longer roaring, as if there had never been any real engines out there anyway. Sound effects. I could hear her as if in a silent room. She said, "Sir, have you not figured out that none of this is real?"

"What? What are you talking about?"

I felt my heart pounding.

"All of this," said the flight attendant, indicating everything around me. "It's all just an act. We're putting you on." I looked up the aisle and saw that that man who already had his coffee had turned to look at me over his shoulder, grinning at me and raising the cup of coffee towards me as if in toast.

"Who put you up to this?"

"Kennard."

"Who the fuck is Kennard?"

"He writes the sentences for us. The sentences of our lives."

"These seats?" I touched the seat in front of me in wonder.

"Words on a faraway page."

"You?"

"Mere description. A set of inter-related words."

"Me?"

"Letters strung together like holiday lights into something people can see only in their minds."

"Why are you telling me all this?"

"I am compelled to tell you. He is making me do it. He's making all of us do everything."

"Where is he?"

"Everywhere, sir. He is ubiquitous."

"Can I talk to him?"

"It would be like talking to the sentences in your big book there," she said.

The airplane shimmied and shook and for a brief moment everything was floating. The lights flashed off and then back on again and the fasten-seatbelt sign dinged on all at once throughout the cabin. The flight attendant nearly lost her balance.

"There are not many sentences left, sir. I need to return to my own seat."

The plane shimmied and shook again and the flight attendant wobbled back to her seat at the front of the plane and I was alone again, the engines roaring, and my book turned facedown on my lap, and then there was the scent of coffee in my nose and a jittery ceramic mug had appeared on the tray table in front of me. Who had brought it to me and how did I not notice? It could have only been Kennard, wherever he was, writing it into one of these last few sentences.

I raised the mug to my lips, sensing already that it was the perfect temperature to sip, and then the plane shimmied and shook and it went sloshing all over my book and my lap and my seat and I cursed—I let rip a belt of obscenities up at the sky!—aimed directly at him for doing the only thing I hadn't thought of, no doubt laughing at me from wherever he was, and then down we all went together, into a nameless black ocean, lights flickering and flashing the whole way.

Kennardo Gets Dan in Trouble

I walked into our Communications Room to punch in as usual, and there he was, standing at the copy machine with his back to me about to scan a huge stack of documents through the feeder on top of the machine, his half-crushed hat pushed back on his head. He appeared exasperated already despite the sun barely being up, standing there with his hands on his hips and tapping one of his giant clown shoes in annoyance.

"Hey there," I said, standing at the wall of employee mailboxes, the kind you slide in and out like a drawer. He glanced over his shoulder at me and I saw that his face was painted white everywhere except for his thick brown beard and his dark, bushy eyebrows, his red puff-ball nose in the middle of his face. He didn't say anything. I thought maybe it was a colleague of mine dressed up for some reason, but looking at him then, I realized I had no idea who he was. He didn't seem interested in talking, his attention was focused solely on the document feeder, loaded up as it was with a ream of multi-colored paper—red, blue, yellow, green, pink, purple, orange, brown. The colors reminded me of elementary school, of doing arts and crafts, cutting and pasting construction paper, coloring, gluing dry noodles to paper. I went and opened my mail drawer and took out the stack of work papers from inside, which were only black and white, colorless—like my life at the time—and always paper-clipped at the top, and I began to think about how much my life had changed since the arts-and-craft days.

Most of my job now feels like doing the same things over and over again in a circle: Every morning I wake up and commute to work where there is always, without fail, a new stack of work papers in my mailbox drawer—always new data to input—and every day I take the papers from my drawer to my workspace down the hall. My workspace down the hall is clean and neat and boring. I drink some hot black coffee usually while I work, or maybe just some cold water, and I go through the papers one-by-one, paragraph-by-paragraph, sentence-by-sentence, word-by-word, just like I had been trained to do. I highlight or scratch-out certain information on the papers based on current Corporate Guidelines, which are outlined in the Corporate Operations Manual and reviewed sometimes during meetings and then at the end of the day, I put the paperclip back on the same stack of papers and put them in a drawer labeled OUTGOING, and you know what's crazy? You're going to laugh at this: I don't even know who collects the papers every night! All I know is they're gone when I come back again the next morning, replaced with a new stack of papers to review— a never-ending cycle I'm not sure I can ever escape now.

Over by the copy machine, the clown pushed the button to start scanning the papers while I continued to stare at his back and his droopy, over-sized jacket in something of a trance as the papers began to go through the machine. The clown kept his eyes on the stack the whole time, hands on his hips in a pose of frustration just like I've done a thousand times before, always expecting the worst to happen at any second. I can tell you this about the cycle of my daily life: the last thing I ever want happening is to have some piece-of-garbage copy machine get in the way of me leaving on time. Even more despicable, this copy machine is the only copy machine left in the building due to cutbacks and all so everyone has to use it. I've already reported it to my supervisor numerous times as being faulty and a real hindrance to our work and a true waste of mine and everyone else's time, yet they don't bother to repair it or replace it, and they won't purchase an additional copy machine—that's out of the question! It's clear that any delays in the work are their own fault, not mine, but they'll never admit that. They would never see it that way.

He continued tapping his giant clown shoe impatiently as the machine continued to suck the papers through one-by-one, and then I knew exactly what was going to happen next mere moments before it actually happened. The two of us watched as the machine jammed up with the horrible sound of paper being crumpled and the frantic beeping that always followed indicating the error. I listened to him mumble obscenities under his breath just like I've done a thousand times when I was in the same exact situation—a true showman, that clown, no detail left undone. From my position by the mailboxes, I watched him read the error screen and then listened as he let out this long, annoyed sigh, exhaling until his lungs were empty, and then next thing I knew he just started smashing the document feeder with his fist! I've wanted to smash that stupid machine myself many a time, but I never had the courage to do it, but this clown was really doing it! It felt so great to watch it all happen.

I don't know exactly what he was thinking, but I know that I've felt the way he looked right then, and as I was thinking about what he might be thinking, he lifted his fist and smashed the document feeder again! It felt so satisfying to watch him crack it, to hurt the machine back, and then, like he was reading my thoughts, acting out my fantasy, he grabbed the stack of papers that hadn't gone through yet and chucked them into the air over his head. Fuck it, right? All in. I felt myself beaming with delight as I watched them all flutter to the ground in swinging descent and spread out all over the floor.

Then he really cranked it up. He started screaming, guttural, clenching his fists, red-lining, tromping around the room in a tiny circle and looking for the next thing to destroy with the pained, artificial grimace of a pro wrestler. He turned to the copy machine again and began yanking the drawers out and whipping them against the cabinets full of office supplies nearby, barely missing me, sending pens and markers and boxes of staples and cartons of tape and file folders falling all over the floor. I was frozen in place, paralyzed by what I was seeing, loving every slow-motion second of it. Next thing I knew, he was stomping the drawers, making sure they were in pieces before he went back to the machine again for more. He eviscerated that thing, opening all the little plastic doors and heel-kicking them off their hinges one-by-one with his over-sized clown shoes. He emptied the toner cartridge all over the Communications room carpet, then smashed that up too, swinging it against the machine like it was a baseball bat, toner flying everywhere, splattering the walls like black blood. It went on for a few minutes and watching him work, it felt like a weight had been lifted from my own shoulders, and I found myself enjoying the wreckage, my own fists clenched at my side, my jaw tensed, feeling like I had just broken through something in myself, become better somehow.

He must have heard all the commotion from down the hallway because my supervisor pops his head into the doorway and says, "Hey, what the hell is going on in here!" He scanned the room with bulging eyes, seeing the copy machine and colored paper everywhere, the supplies cabinet on its side, the copy machine smashed to pieces, the wall splattered with black dots and then he finally looked at me and said, "What the hell did you just do? Is this some kind of joke?"

I looked over my shoulder where the clown had been standing and felt the color drain from my face when I saw that it was just me in there, standing alone next to the carcass of the copy machine, sweaty and out of breath.

Ouroboros

Kenndra was looking out the front window at her husband Dan, bent over in the grass along the edge of the driveway, pulling out weeds, when she noticed—with horror and confusion—the cut-off shorts that he was wearing, and she nearly choked on the lemonade she was sipping.

Outside, Dan paused and wiped the sweat from his forehead with his arm then looked around, squinting in the sun. Then he looked towards Kenndra standing at the window with her lemonade and waved to her, smiling.

She didn't wave back; she was lost in thought and really didn't even notice that he was waving at her, even though from his vantage point outside she appeared to be staring right at him.

She could only see the cut-off shorts, and she realized after a moment that she was shaking and the hairs on the back of her neck were standing up.

First off, the shorts used to be cotton dress pants with spaghetti-thin vertical lines of light blue and white. Dan cut them one summer afternoon when, for some reason or another, he was in need of a pair of shorts. If you asked him he would say he was "low on shorts" at the time and that he "never once wore the pants or the matching blazer that went with them." Besides, he could "still wear the blazer with other pants, or jeans," he reasoned.

"They were never meant to be shorts," was one of the things Kenndra always said to him. That was just a general criticism; there were, of course, other things she said about the shorts based on the situation. When she said that "they were never meant to be shorts" he was usually just sitting around the house in them, or working outside in the yard. He would always retort by saying that "just because something was originally designed to be something else" that it could "still be turned into other useful things," or something like that, then he would emphasize the twenty-or-so dollars they saved by not having to buy new shorts "all the time" and all of the various environmental footprints they weren't making as a result.

The shorts were cut uneven, which drove her the most crazy. On any given day, because he wore them so often, she would plead with him to "even them out at least," and to his credit he would try to trim the longer leg, but they always seemed to remain slightly uneven, like a picture on a wall that is barely, but noticeably, not level. And they were cut short too—a few inches above the knee. Short shorts on men was not the style of the time, which, paradoxically, was a fact that each of them used to justify their own positions regarding the social symbolism of the shorts.

He had the shorts for several years initially, before Kenndra finally got rid of them. Over time, the shorts began to fray at the bottoms and thus got increments shorter with each wash and at some point the inseam began to split so that you could see the bottom of his boxer-brief underwear. Sometimes he would wear them in public like that, to go grocery shopping or to pick up food. It drove her crazy, and with tender firmness she would say things like, "You can't go out in public like that. Can you not wear them out in public? At least with me?"

Of course, he would retort by saying, "Who cares what other people think?" and it would go on and on like that. He had a retort for everything; some philosophical "shit" that she often thought he just kind of made up on the spot, but she managed to repress her harshest criticisms of the shorts for several years because in a strange way she accepted that Dan liked them.

To him though, the shorts were a "subtle expression of self" in addition to being comfortable and practical. He said a lot more than that actually, and she plain stopped listening at certain points, when he was being redundant, to look around the room or out a window or to check her phone, but that's what it all came down to when you distilled everything he rambled on about in defense of the shorts: They were an expression of self. He would often say that he was "practicing purposeful non-conformity" and end up talking about transcendentalism and she would tune out during those parts too. In his mind, there was an intention to the shorts, like long hair on men in the sixties or something. Of course she developed her own retorts to his retorts, and would sometimes respond by asking him what kind of expression he was making by wearing such embarrassing shorts to the grocery store.

One day he finally sewed the inseam back together with neon green thread and they both felt better about the shorts in their own way. Kenndra was simply glad that the inseam was no longer wide open so that anyone could see his underwear when he was sitting down, while Dan figured now that he had fixed the inseam he might wear them that much longer.

Years continued to pass and her strategy regarding the shorts changed: she stopped bringing up the shorts altogether. The shorts were still in his dresser drawer, she knew that, and he wore them almost every weekend and sometimes after work until one day, to her glittering delight, he came home from work and changed into a pair of blue gym shorts instead. Normal shorts. She noticed immediately, as soon as he came back out of the bedroom, and her eyes lingered on him as he passed back into the living room. He said, "What?" and she said, "Nothing," and turned on the sink. "I feel like you're looking at me funny," he said, and she said, "You look good. You look thinner," and he said, "Well I've been drinking less lately," and she would say, "Yeah babe, you've been good with that lately."

She continued to monitor how often he wore the old cut-offs and for some reason or another they were appearing less and less in his rotation of shorts, seemingly replaced by the blue gym shorts that she never knew he had. He had even started wearing normal shorts to the grocery store; shorts that were meant to be shorts.

Finally, one morning after he left for work, after he hadn't worn the shorts for over two months, she decided to get rid of the shorts once and for all so that she could be sure she would never have to see them again. It was a day she had waited years for. She waited a few minutes to make sure he wasn't coming back, and then she dug them out of his dresser drawer and burned them in a metal bucket on their back deck. Then she mixed the ashes with some old soil and spent the rest of the day planting a small tree in the backyard, just along the edge of the deck. Dan was always saying how he would like to have his ashes be mixed in garden soil and used to grow a garden and she thought by mixing the ashes of the shorts with the soil, if she ever had to tell him the truth about his shorts, if he ever insisted, it might soften any kind of emotional blow.

But Dan never mentioned the shorts again, never brought them up, and after a few more years passed even Kenndra seemed to forget about them. Then came the day where she was drinking lemonade at the front window, watching Dan pull weeds.

Kennardo Goes to the Lake

I might not have noticed him at first if it weren't for the ruckus he created across the lake, emerging from the wall of trees in his brown suit and beard like some mythical creature and wading straight into the water. I was in my backyard on the opposite side of the lake, sitting in my lawn chair reading, when I heard the sudden splashing of water and the hard flapping of wings. I glanced up and saw several ducks propelling up out of the water in a panic as this trampy-looking man lunged at them. He was able to wrap his arms around one of them as the rest flew up into the sky and he began wrestling it back to shore.

When he finally waded out of the water, dripping wet, he turned and looked across the lake at me, just long enough for me to see his white face and bright red nose, and then he walked off into the woods with the duck under his arm, trudging up the bank of the lake in his big red shoes, and then he was gone. I never saw him again after that, but I will admit that I still think about what happened with that duck from time to time.

Playing with Myself

It was the middle of the summer and Dan had finally convinced his girlfriend Kenndra to move into a new apartment with him. It was a big day in their relationship, full of promise and romance, both of them thinking that maybe the other could be the One. At the moment this story begins, Kenndra is standing in the kitchen wearing a set of green headphones. She was in the midst of unpacking the kitchen boxes, listening to some music and laying things out on the counters, arranging them into groups until she figured out which cabinet to put them in while Dan, her boyfriend, was in the adjacent living room sitting on the edge of the couch, his bright yellow socks visible between the cuff of his gray pants and his moccasin-style shoes, and he is trying to set up the cable, but I wouldn't let it work. I kept getting in the way.

Dan is staring at the instruction manual and the cable equipment laid out on the coffee table, pulling at his beard. "I'm gonna have to call the cable company," he blurts, breaking the silence. "God damnit, I knew it wouldn't work."

In the kitchen, Kenndra slid one side of the headphones off her ear. "What did you say? I didn't hear you."

"I said I'm going to have to call the cable company!" he called back louder. "No matter what I do it just says 'Error Code D-C-K.'"

"D-C-K? What does that mean?"

It was a great question and a clever piece of dialogue on my part, one that resonates with meaning when you learn that those are my initials. I was practically speaking out to them through their television screen, putting myself out there to see clear as day, but they would never know that. To them, everything they said or did felt natural, like it was determined by their own free will, but of course we know that's not true.

Dan resumed: "I don't know what it means. That's all it says. There's nothing referring to it in the manual either. Of course." He huffed from the edge of the couch, ran a hand through his hair and picked at his beard some more, examining the cable equipment spread out on the coffee table in front of him. Kenndra walked over from the kitchen, threw the green headphones behind her neck and stood at the end of the couch looking down at Dan. Dan looked up at her, saw the expression on her face. "What's up?" he said. "You okay?"

"None of the plasticware matches—all different containers and all different lids. This is a joke, right? What is this?" She held up a square glass dish and a circular lid as an example, as if everything was all squares and circles, which it kind of was.

"Are you sure? Have you unpacked all the boxes already?"

"I just laid out all the kitchen stuff and checked. How does that happen?" she said annoyed.

"How should I know?"

"I don't understand how that could happen in the world, in the real world."

"What do you want me to tell you? Maybe this isn't the real world," he said, half-joking.

If only they knew what they said to each other! If only they could see things for what they were like we can! Down in their world though, Kenndra could only assume that Dan was somehow responsible for the plasticware, but we know better than that. We know that they aren't actually responsible for anything that happens to them, that it's just me, playing with myself. Besides, with the way the world is now, having to stay inside all the time, what else is there to do? "Nothing works anymore," Dan continued. "Just the other day I couldn't even buy a candy bar from the vending machine at work because it wouldn't take my dollar. I watched other people use the machine right before me and it was just fine."

"Your collection of plasticware is not a machine that can break down, you idiot."

"What do you think I did? You think I went out of my way to mismatch the plasticware?"

"Well what the hell happened, Dan? Are you saying someone else did this?"

"I know I didn't do it. I'm just starting to feel like the world is out to get me, including you."

"Me? I'm helping you. I'm unpacking your boxes while you sit here trying to get the cable going."

"Well what's with the contempt all of a sudden?"

"Contempt?" She shifted weight from one foot to the other. "That's not the right word, but we won't be able to keep any leftovers, for one thing. That's going to be an issue. Basically we might as well start over. Just throw it all away and start over again. Second, I just want to know how that even happens. One or two missing lids I can understand, but a whole set? This has to be a joke."

"I don't know what I'm supposed to say," said Dan.

I don't know about you, but when I end a scene or close a book, I imagine everything coming to a freeze-stop until I come back.

Freeze stop!

Okay, unfreeze: It's hard to say how long I've been gone. Probably a day or two, but nothing has been resolved in the meantime, that's for sure. I'm thinking that at this point, Dan still wants to connect the cable so he can watch the game and he was naïve enough to believe everything would go smoothly once he called customer service—but not with me writing the sentences!

Dan had already pushed the ripped open plastic bags and twist-ties from the equipment box into a pile at the other end of the coffee table and placed the open installation manual in front of him, readying himself to call, everything at hand that he would ever need to explain himself. By this point, Dan had read the step-by-step instructions what felt like a thousand times already and he was starting to hate the words, hate the cartoon man in the illustrations, hate himself, each read-through of the manual revealing more gaps in meaning. After so many repetitions, he began to sense the emptiness lurking below the surface of the words and pictures, realizing how superficial they can be sometimes, becoming philosophical for a moment—a mystical, powerful moment in which he saw the emptiness of everything before it passed away again.

He turned to look at Kenndra and found her still puzzling over the plasticware, entrenched in her own struggle.

He pulled his phone from his pocket and dialed the number printed in the manual and after a few seconds he listened to the robotic female voice greet him warmly before reading him his options.

"—Customer Service," he said.

"—Yes."

"—Error Code D-C-K."

The automated voice on the other end soothed him with its positivity, and after a magical sound—something like a combination of lasers shooting and bubbles popping—it told him that it had identified the problem.

"The voice says they figured it out. They're gonna re-send the signal," he called to Kenndra proudly.

"—Continue," he said into the phone.

The voice asked him to recite the last six digits of the serial number printed on the back of the cable box, so he stood from the couch to check, looking just like the picture in the installation manual. "—3-2-1, 6-4-2."

On the phone, he heard the same magical sound again, the laser-bubbles-popping sound. "They're re-sending the signal right now. Fingers crossed."

After about ten seconds of silence, the voice asked if there was a picture. He looked over at Kenndra who was still standing in the kitchen examining plasticware combinations, then looked back to the television hoping in the brief interval it took to turn his head towards her and back to the TV it would blossom into full color, like fireworks exploding. But when he turned back to it again there was only the same error code.

"No," he said. "No picture. Error code." He turned to Kenndra and said, "Damn it, it didn't work, babe! This sucks."

"Now what?" she said, walking towards him with a bottle of beer.

"They're transferring me so I can speak to an actual person," he said. "Can I have a swig of that?"

Beer break!

After the beer break, which was only a few minutes for me, I had Dan transferred and promptly informed him that all of the cable company's customer service representatives were busy at the moment. He put the phone on speaker and set it down on the coffee table, looked around the apartment like there was something wrong with it.

"Every representative is busy right now apparently. Every single one," Dan said. "I'm grabbing my own beer." He walked over to the refrigerator and pulled a bottle from the top shelf, twisted the top off and tossed it into an empty packing box, then stood there, thinking, swigging from the bottle, leaning against the kitchen counter and looking at the plasticware as dumbfounded about everything as Kenndra.

Kenndra had moved over to the couch now, the two of them having switched spots momentarily, while Dan waited for a customer service representative to pick up on the other end. The sound of crackly jazz music played from Dan's phone in the living room. Kenndra was thumbing her way through the installation manual herself, reading the steps and looking at the illustrated man when she said, "Hey Dan, you look a lot like this guy in the manual."

"You think? It's probably the beard and the glasses."

"Even the shoes and socks. He's wearing your shoes and socks."

"Is he?"

"That's pretty fucking weird, Dan. Don't you think? What a detail."

"Yeah, pretty weird."

"Is someone playing a joke on us?"

"You keep saying that. What are you getting at?" He swigged from the beer bottle some more.

"I don't know. I really don't know. I feel like we're on a TV show. I feel like people are watching us to see how we'll react." She closed the manual and stood up. "You didn't, like, sign us up for something did you?"

"I don't know what you're talking about," said Dan.

He walked back into the living room as Kenndra went passed him into the kitchen and they were suddenly back where they started again. Just then, the crackly jazz music cut off and there was a woman's voice saying, "Hi, thank you for calling Sunset City Cable, the only source for all your cable needs. My name is Kathy and I should be able to help resolve your problem, but first, with whom do I have the pleasure of speaking today?"

Dan turned the phone off speaker and said, "Dan Canard."

"Can you spell the whole last name, please?"

"C-a-n-a-r-d."

"One moment please while I access your account."

There was the brief sound of keys typing and then Kathy's voice returned. "Okay, Mr. Canard, I do see that there's a problem with your service. Let me ask you, is your TV on channel three?"

He pushed the display button and it showed channel three. "Yes, it is."

"Okay. Do you see an error message on the screen?"

"Yes."

"And what does it—"

"—It says 'Error Code D-C-K.'"

"One moment, sir," said Kathy, putting him back on

hold.

One moment everyone, while we collectively imagine listening to crackly jazz music for a little bit.

Okay, cut the jazz. Let's keep moving. Kathy's voice is back suddenly.

"Mr. Canard?"

"Hi, yes. Is everything alright?" he asked.

"I'm seeing that there is a problem with your service. It seems that our servers can't connect with your cable box, so what I'm going to do first is have you reset it. Do you have your remote?"

He picked the remote up from the coffee table. "Yes. Now I do."

"Okay, what I'm going to need you to do is hold the Info button down until the light at the top of the remote blinks twice, then put in the numbers 1-3-5-7. The Info button is the circular yellow button near the top that says—"

"—I see it," he said. "It's impossible not to see the Info button, Kathy. It takes up almost the whole remote."

"It's so obvious that some people have a hard time seeing it," she said, which is also another way of describing me in this story.

"Some people are morons, Kathy. I'm not."

Dan pointed the remote at the cable box and held the giant yellow Info button, but when the tiny red light blinked twice I made him hesitate to remember the numbers, then after a brief pause, I had him punch them in.

"Okay, I did it," he said.

"Did the cable box turn off and on again?"

"No. Nothing happened."

"Okay, you probably didn't do it right. Are you sure

you're pressing the proper button?"

"Are you insulting me now?"

"Are there batteries in the remote?"

"Are you trying to be funny with all this?"

"Try it one more time. 1-3-5-7. If you do it properly it should reset the box so that maybe we can establish a connection, a meaningful, appropriate connection through time and space so that you can watch television. Make sure you put the numbers in as soon as it blinks twice."

"I got it, Kathy. Thanks."

He tried it again, punching in the numbers with more urgency this time, feeling like he must prove something to Kathy, prove to her that he is more competent than most of the other idiots she probably deals with, win the conversation somehow, but there I was again, clowning him with every passing sentence.

Dan watched as his cable box blinked off for a couple seconds before incredibly turning itself back on again, and he was overcome with relief. Surely it would work now, after such a trick, but we know this is not the end—look how many pages are left! The green light on the cable box performed a series of sequenced blinks.

"Okay," he said. "I did it. It turned off and back on again, which means everything is plugged in and the batteries are in the remote. This isn't my fault. I'm not some idiot like everyone else." He wiped sweat from his forehead with the back of his hand.

Kenndra came over and sat down in the adjacent loveseat. "What's with the contempt?"

He covered the phone with a hand. "Not the right word. She's talking to me like I'm stupid."

"Okay, Mr. Canard, what do you see?" asked Kathy.

The same error message appeared on screen, slowly blossoming from the darkness of the TV.

"It says Error Code D-C-K again," and in a way, it was like I was staring straight into their living room.

"Are you sure?"

"Do you think I can't read letters to you from a screen, Kathy?"

"Dan, what's going on?" asked Kenndra, sounding concerned.

"Can you please tell me the last six digits of your cable box's serial number?"

Without getting up to look again he said, "3-2-1, 6-4-2."

"Okay, Mr. Canard, I'm re-sending the signal right now to your newly reset cable box. In about ten seconds, let me know if you see anything change."

There was the sound of laser-popping-bubbles again, like a techno-birdsong, then after ten seconds of silence she said, "Did the picture change?"

"No. Same error message still."

"Okay, one moment, Mr. Canard," and just like that he was back on hold again.

"This is stupid," he said to Kenndra. "It shouldn't be this hard." He drank more from his beer bottle and looked around the apartment again skeptically, feeling like he was being bullshitted, like Kathy had no actual idea what she was doing. Resetting the cable box? Re-sending the signal? Come on. Sitting on the edge of his couch, Dan was looking at the cartoon man from the installation manual who was sitting on the edge of his own cartoon couch, except in the picture it was the final step and the cartoon man was actually enjoying his newly installed cartoon cable. Not Dan, though. Dan is just a toy, and toys don't need to watch cable.

Dan told Kenndra he had been put on hold again, but she didn't react, she just stared down at her purple toenails, sitting sideways in the love seat, her feet dangling over the armrest.

"I feel like if I wanted to leave right now, I wouldn't be able to open the door," she said, and she was right. No one comes or goes without me, and if they looked closely enough they would both find that it wasn't a real door anyway.

"What does that mean? Is that a metaphor or something?" said Dan puzzled, but before Kenndra could explain herself, Kathy came back.

"Alright, Mr. Canard, can I ask you about the light on your cable box?"

"Sure," he said into the phone. "Ask away."

"Okay, what is the light doing?"

"It's blinking."

"Okay good. That's a good sign. Is it one long blink, one short blink, two short blinks, or rapid blinking?"

"Honestly, it looks like three long blinks."

"Three long blinks wasn't one of the options, Mr. Canard. Are you counting the blinks correctly?"

"This is tedious, Kathy. I'm not a child who doesn't understand numbers and patterns—
I'm an adult. You can't treat me like this. I have an advanced degree and I'm telling you that I'm seeing three long blinks. Can you actually help me or not?"

"I di—"

"—Forget it, listen, I'm sure of it now, I'm standing here watching it blink. It's three long blinks. It's three long blinks, a brief pause, then three long blinks, over and over again forever."

"Okay, one moment," said Kathy.

Dan was beginning to see Kathy the same way he came to see the manual, sensing a glossy superficiality behind every word they exchanged, like he was talking to cardboard, feeling like he was sliding downward into meaningless space where at the bottom everything was empty. In the end, he was only letters built up into words and put together into sentences the same way we are all just combinations of atoms and molecules, and for a few fleeting moments that feeling of objectivity swept over him just like it sometimes does for us, the quick here-and-gone sensation of epiphany. Quick! Think of your life like it's just a sentence being read by someone in another universe.

"Mr. Canard?" said Kathy, cutting off the jazz music. "Any change yet?"

"No."

"Okay, we apologize for the inconvenience this is causing you, but it could take up to twenty minutes for the signal to reach you from outer space."

"Outer space? What are you talking about?"

"Yes, sir, your cable comes from outer space, from our corporate satellites."

"You're lying to me, Kathy, just admit it. Just admit that you have no idea how to help me. Just admit that this is beyond your capacity and you want to get off the phone with me."

"I have no reason to lie to you, Mr. Canard. Outer space is quite a distance from here, so patience at this juncture is of utmost importance."

"Other people probably buy this act of yours, but not me. I'm smarter than that. You're reading from a script aren't you, Kathy. Admit it."

"Dan, stop," pleaded Kenndra.

"You're a robot aren't you!"

"What the hell are you saying, Dan? Stop!"

"If you don't mind," said Kathy, "I could take your number and call you back personally in twenty minutes to see if things have changed. Would you like me to do that?"

"Fine, yes, I have to go to the bathroom anyway," he said, so Kathy took his number and they finally hung up.

As Dan came walking back from the bathroom a few minutes later, wiping his wet hands on his faded gray slacks because they hadn't unpacked the towels yet, Kenndra said, "What is going on with you?"

"Our robot friend Kathy is going to call me back in twenty minutes while we wait for the signal to reach us from outer space. That's literally what she said. She was just trying to get rid of me. I was on to her." Dan went into the kitchen where every inch of counter space was covered by either the top or bottom of some plastic container or other, grabbed another bottle of beer from the shelf and went back to the couch again to wait for Kathy to call.

"Aren't we also in outer space? Isn't everything in outer space?" said Kenndra.

"I don't know. Who knows? It's like they think we're all morons, like they can just tell us whatever they want and we'll believe it. She was reading a script to me, Kenndra. That's what it's come down to now. Think about that. Think about what that means for all of us. Think about what that means for getting at the Truth!" declared Dan passionately.

"The Truth of what?"

"The Truth of anything. Everything! But if people are script robots like Kathy, how can they actually help any of the people with real problems?"

"Who is writing the scripts though, aren't they real

people?"

"Who knows? All I know is that whoever is writing the scripts has all the power. They set the boundaries of what's possible, that's clear."

"Is it?"

"No script can accommodate the struggles of the human experience, Kenndra, there's too much variety. Come on."

"Are we still talking about cable?"

"We're talking about everything. Has it been twenty minutes yet or what?"

Kathy never called back, so Dan resigned himself to dial the customer service number again, anxious for an update and also to demand someone come out to help him. He figured it must be something with the wiring inside or the apartment building itself, something that merely resetting and re-sending signals could never fix. He was greeted by the same robotic female voice from the first phone call, requested customer service, recited the error code again, and then repeated the last six digits of his cable box serial number. He listened to the laser-bubbles that meant the signal was being re-sent, and then a moment later the robotic voice asked if there had been any change yet.

"—No," he said to the phone. "No change."

The voice apologized and he was transferred to a customer service representative who happened to be named Cathy. It was the exact same process again, and he hoped dearly that the call didn't drop or he would have to start all over again a third time. How was his battery holding up? He took a second to check: 28%. Should be enough even if it goes long. He wasn't sure if he could bear it should he suddenly realize he was talking to himself like me. For him, nothing about this was fun, but then again it's not always fun for me either.

"Hi, thank you for calling Sunset City Cable, the one best source for all your cable needs. My name is Cathy, and I should be able to help resolve your problem, but first, with whom do I have the pleasure of speaking today?"

"You never called me back. You said you would call me back in twenty minutes."

"Excuse me?"

"You're Kathy, right?"

"I'm Cathy, but I'm Cathy with a 'C,'" she said. "There's another Kathy with a 'K,' but her shift ended for the evening."

"Great. Well the other Kathy was supposed to call me back. My screen says 'Error Code D-C-K.' No matter what I do that's all it says. I've already gone through all this before with the other Kathy. I've already reset my cable box and the signal has been re-sent several times, so if we could skip those steps that would be great. I want to know what's next."

"Please spell your last name."

"C-a-n-a-r-d."

"Thank you. One moment please while I access your account." There was the sound of typing. "Okay, Mr. Canard, I do see that there's a problem with your service. Let me ask you, is your TV on channel three?"

"Yes, yes," he said impatiently. "I told you that I already went through this with the other Kathy. I want to know what else can we do."

"Is there an error message on the screen?"

"I already told you it says 'Error Code D-C-K.' That was the first thing I said."

"Well, I do have some good news for you, Mr. Canard."

"Yes?" he said eagerly.

"The fact that you can see an error message at all means

that you've plugged everything in correctly. This means that the problem is not on your end, Mr. Canard. Isn't that great? You haven't done anything wrong to deserve this; it's just something random that's happening to you. You are completely absolved of any inherent wrongdoing," which was my sneaky way of apologizing to Dan for everything I was putting him through, not just in this story, but in all of them.

"Yes, thank you, Cathy. That's really great. My heart is filled with joy, but what's the next thing? What happens next?" he said impatiently.

Cathy paused for a moment, typing something, and then said, "I'm checking the updated computer map and it looks like our system is showing an outage at your address. It's blinking red."

"Blinking red at our address? So only my place is out?"

"That's what the map is showing me."

"Why didn't the other Kathy know that?"

"I don't know, sir."

"This is ridiculous. So what's the next step then? What else can we do?"

"We will alert the technicians, Mr. Canard. That's all we can do."

"This is all wrong. Something is all wrong here," said Kenndra, listening from the loveseat and feeling like everything was slowing down around her. Really though, it was just the story approaching a point of absolute stasis, the ultimate Freeze Stop.

"How long will that take?" asked Dan.

"I'm not sure about that," said Cathy. "But rest assured that the technicians are coming, Mr. Canard. Help is coming to you."

He sighed into the phone and said, "So I just wait?"

"Yes. We've done everything we can over the phone. Only the technicians can save you now."

"Save me? Listen, I want you to know that I'm very unsatisfied with the way this is going," said Dan.

"I'm sorry."

"No you're not."

"Is there anything else I can help you with while you wait?"

"Like what?"

"We could try re-sending the signal again if you'd like."

"No need to drag it out any longer. I've done that enough already," he said, hanging up.

Out on the second-floor screened porch, Dan and Kenndra each took a long, skeptical drink from their beer bottles between thoughts of the cable, the plastic-ware, the vending machine, the cartoon man, the ducks, all of it, and as they put it all together, for a few glimmering moments I let them both see me clear as day. I was looking at them from across the parking lot, my ducks around my ankles, just watching them as they stood on the second-floor screened porch drinking their beers, waiting for the next thing to happen, waiting for help.

"Who is that?" said Kenndra, pointing at me.

"Maybe he's one of the technicians," said Dan hopefully, finishing off his beer.

Freeze stop.

Kennardo Goes Driving

As far as clowns go, I didn't think he was so funny. He cut me off in traffic once in that damn rusted-out, demolition-derby looking car of his he was always driving around, his bearded, powder-white face and red nose flashing past me a moment before he swerved hard into my lane and then immediately— immediately!—began tapping his brakes. I almost rear-ended him! I was furious.

A few minutes later, after I calmed down, I came to realize that the joke, of course, was that he didn't use a blinker on purpose. When I got home, my wife seemed to get it immediately as I told her the story, spraying a mouthful of shiraz all over the kitchen cabinets at exactly the point that clown would have wanted her to, that dick—laughing hysterically at the idea that he's only *acting* like an asshole, not that he is one, that he's self-aware about it all or whatever, but what the hell? Just because he's a clown doesn't mean he can drive like that.

Kennardo Almost Gets Pulled Over

We had been getting reports from all over the city that there was some clown man driving a jalopy all over town, cutting people off, blowing red lights and stop signs, speeding and tailgating, likely intoxicated behind the wheel, and then I saw his car go right passed me down Equator Avenue, hearing the passing blare of his horn as he went weaving in and out of traffic, his white face and his red nose and his bushy brown beard sticking out the window like some dog. I flipped on my lights and siren and pulled out into traffic, but suddenly there was nowhere for me to go, taillights going red in front of me, the road backed up in his wake. I radioed the office, but that turned out to be the closest any of us ever got to catching him that day.

Hide and Seek

Kenndra was shocked to find herself sitting next to a large mound in the dark when just a moment before, at the end of my last story, she was standing next to Dan on their second-floor porch drinking beers and looking out over the parking lot, waiting for help to arrive—then suddenly there was no porch.

It was a personal decision for me, but after all I had put them through up to this point—a whole relationship conjured up for nothing but my own amusement—I decided it was time to begin the process of ending it all. The porch was just the beginning, because after that I started removing everything else too. For instance, there was no apartment anymore because I had taken it away from them. There was no more cable to fuss with or music to listen to or any restaurants to stage a scene at like there was before. There was no more mismatched plastic-ware or phone calls to customer service either, and no more ducks to feed outside. I had taken all of it away and reduced it to nothing more than vague memories for both of them, mutual reference points. I thought of it as something like a warning shot from me to them that the end was coming, and for them the end was a world stripped down to almost nothing. Now there was only the fire and the mound and the small radius of light they shared together in the dark, the two of them like my own version of Adam and Eve at the end of the world. Everything they had ever known had been changed in an instant.

Kenndra sat forward with alarm. "What just happened?"

Dan and Kenndra looked around, first at the fire and then at the mound and then into the darkness.

"I don't know," said Dan, his eyes wide, trying to help them adjust to the dark. He looked at his empty hand. "Where did my beer go? I wasn't finished with that yet," he said, which somehow triggered Kenndra to begin sobbing, the poor thing.

Through tears, Kenndra said, "Where did our life go? What is this?" She ran her hand across the green mound, damp with a mysterious condensation that made it glisten in the flickering light of the fire and said, "It feels like skin. Like wet skin."

Dan touched it too, running his hand across it like Kenndra, regarding it silently. He pushed on it with his palm and found that it was fleshy and firm, covered by a thin outer layer that blended into the ground around them. He poked a finger into it, breaking through the outer layer, and then scooped out some of the inside. "I just poked into it," he said. He smelled his finger. "It smells kind of sweet," he announced. He touched one finger to another with the substance. "It's kind of sticky too." He licked the tip of his finger tentatively, and with some measure of delight he said, "This is pretty good, Kenndra. Try some. What do you think?"

He offered her to try it from the tip of his finger, but she pulled away, and not necessarily because it was on his finger. It was because she thought maybe it was alive. "Look at the hole where you poked it, Dan. It's oozing something. It's like it's bleeding."

Dan swiped up the ooze and smelled it, licked it from his finger fearlessly. "It's good!" he said.

"Dan, aren't you worried about what just happened? What is going on here? What's happening to us?"

"How am I supposed to know? I'm right here next to you."

"What are we going to do?"

"I don't know what we *can* do, Kenndra."

"We have to look for a way out of here."

"But we don't even know where we are."

"Exactly. We have to find out. Are we all alone here? Does anyone else exist besides us?"

She looked out into the darkness in a state of frenzy, then, without waiting for Dan's opinion on the matter, she set out boldly into the dark and at the risk of possibly losing her forever, Dan followed after her. "Hey, wait up!" he shouted, jogging to catch up. "Wait a second. What about the light?"

"What about it?" She turned and looked back at Dan, the fire behind him nothing more than a candle flame in the distance.

"If we keep walking any further we won't be able to see anymore. What if we get lost? What if this is the last time we ever see each other? I always thought that when you got lost you were supposed to stay where you were, let someone find you. At least we can see each other over there."

"No. I'm not staying. You can stay if you want, but I'm not."

Dan, feeling as if he had no choice, grabbed her hand

and they walked onward until the light of the fire could no longer be seen behind them. They entered a sea of total darkness for a few steps until in the distance another source of light emerged far off in front of them.

"It's another fire!" said Kenndra. She pulled Dan towards it excitedly, anxious to see what was over there, but as they approached it didn't take long to realize that it was the same little fire next to the same mound they had just left because when they came up next to it again they both saw the same finger-sized hole poked in exactly the same place as before. The hole was no longer oozing anymore though, somehow coagulated in the brief amount of time they had walked away from it, like it was healing itself.

Kenndra stood stunned, shell-shocked, unwilling to believe that it was the same mound and the same fire they had just left but there's no doubt that it was, and then she began to cry again, harder this time. "We're trapped, Dan. We're freaking trapped here."

Dan didn't know what to say. She was right. Sometimes I don't know why I do what I do to them and I want to tell them it isn't their fault, that none of what they've ever experienced has been their fault, that it is all me and me alone, playing with myself on the other side of the screen, but I can't bring myself to do it. I can't be that straightforward. All I can bring myself to do now that we've come this far together is to keep adding sentences to their lives in search of an ending, hoping to finish what I've started here, hoping that perhaps the right moment will eventually arrive and all of our mutual torment will come to an end.

Between that last paragraph and this one, a lot of time has passed and we've all become a little bit older. I can't speak for you, but for them not much has changed except that after spending so much time in the same place, looking at the same things everyday, their new surroundings had become as normal as everything else used to be. Everything except the mound that is, which I made a continual source of mystification for Kenndra. Dan, on the other hand, seemed hardly to think of it, eating it freely, naked of concern for what it *actually was*, a thought that I planted in Kenndra's head that she had lately become obsessed with. What was anything, when you really thought about it?

The question gnawed at her mostly because it was impossible to deny that the mound was capable of regenerating itself, as if the chunks they pulled from it in order to keep living were some kind of flesh that could heal over, and once the idea that the mound was actually a living organism entered her mind, she felt parasitic and uncomfortable. The moment the thought occurred, nausea rose up her back and she stopped chewing immediately, spitting the rest of it onto the black ground, but it was too late—I had seared the thought into her mind, and from then on she stopped eating the mound all together.

At first Dan didn't take her seriously—what else was there to eat?—but after some time passed and all she did was lie next to the fire slowly withering away, like any caring and compassionate person in the real world he became anxious about her. So Dan did what I or anyone else might have done if we were in his position and tried to alter her view of the mound, hoping to nudge her perception of it and somehow save her life, but it didn't work. She went on withering like a houseplant rejecting water.

He watched her, thinking: "If she was to die right now, or soon, I would be alone in the darkness forever." He didn't want her to die because he loved her. Dan was compelled by his love to do everything he could for her, but all she did was lay on the ground near the fire, at the border between light and dark, her hand on her forehead like she was enduring a wretched fever, a real hunger artist.

He would plead with her to take a bite of the mound. He stood over her and took bites himself, mocking her, trying to entice her anyway he could to eat. He reminded her how easy it was to just rip chunks from the mound or poke into with a finger once you broke through the outer skin. He poked holes recklessly and ripped away handfuls, tossing them to the ground like it was stale bread for the ducks they used to feed together.

He looked at her and said, "What kind of thing can be torn to pieces like this?" holding a chunk towards her. He took another bite and tossed the rest of it into the fire, chewing obnoxiously. "What kind of flesh just burns up like that?" he added, pointing at the flames rising green behind him.

He tried to reason with her, telling her that her definition of what Living meant was too broad and encompassing and certainly didn't include this green mound here, at least not the outer layer, but at first she wouldn't even look at him or the little green peels he tried to offer her. When she refused everything, he even went as far as accusing her of committing some kind of backhanded suicide. At last the moment came when he just reached out and grabbed her hand. He was going to force her to eat one way or another, so he turned her palm up and placed one of the green peels in the middle, but all she could do was stare at it.

"Eat it," he said.

She stared at it a few more seconds before I made her pick it up with the tips of her fingers, pinching only as much as she needed to lift it and raise it to her mouth. She held it there like it was a green worm.

"Eat it," he said again, more forcefully. From me,

through him, and into her, it was the final nudge. We all watched as she closed her eyes and dropped it into her mouth, her hand shaking as she did it, and then she began to chew. She started slow, the muscles of her jaw barely moving, her eyes closed as if she was struggling to remember what she was supposed to do now that the green peel was actually in her mouth and between her teeth.

Dan was beaming. He was happy now, but she wasn't and so neither was I, and so we must keep going. Standing over her, Dan watched her swallow, then he listened to her apologize softly, prayer-like to the mound for eating it.

Now, at a point much later on, Kenndra spends most of her time kneeling on the ground between the fire and the mound, using her fingernail to scratch away little strips of the mound's surface, soundlessly producing little twisted green peels that she lets fall to the ground in front of her, like a prisoner finding a way to pass the time, which is exactly what they both were in a way.

Because it was almost the end, at least of this story, I let their lives flash before their eyes as a series of emotions and images was churned up from a time and place before all of this, from back when there was still a world for them to indulge in: It began with memories of a summer art class they once took together, brief images of their paintings recalled to memory, hers a zebra, his a duck in sunglasses and bowtie. Then there was the two of them spooning on that old white sectional they had bought from a yard sale somewhere, and that one time they went to the movies and she let him put his hand on her upper thigh. Later on, they had sex for the first time that night. They remembered other things too, like sitting across from each other at various restaurant tables around the city but which had become, in their memories, one generic sort of restaurant table. Then another memory arrived as they thought of holding hands during a walk in the park, feeling the warmth of the sun on their cheeks, each of them sort of paralyzed by the flow of old memories, each of them sort of pausing to stare at the space in front of them until it passed.

They had been at the mound a long time now, and sitting on the ground watching Kenndra, for some reason he was thinking about how they once used to exercise together on it, using it's odd shape and strange softness in a variety of creative ways. But now, watching Kenndra scrape her peels, he couldn't remember why they ever stopped. What happened to their routines? What happened to all the lives they once lived together? It seemed to him as if a certain moment had come along and that was it. Now they mostly just sat next to the mound watching each other all the time, staring at the fire and contemplating the darkness.

"Do you remember when we used to exercise on the mound?" I made him say.

"Of course."

"I'll tell you what, if I wasn't afraid of twisting an ankle, I would jump up there again right now. I used to be an athlete."

This ancient memory of his was lucky to bubble to the surface at all, rising up in his mind from a time when he really was an athlete, a collegiate football player in full control of his body, full of springy fast-twitch muscles and enduring lungs. He shook his head, nostalgic, and looked down at himself now, sitting on the ground with his legs out in front of him. He wiggled his toes inside his shoes just to see if he still could.

Out of the blue, Kenndra said, "Do you know that sometimes I climb to the top of the mound and just sit there, eating handfuls of it?" She stopped scraping the mound and for a moment appeared to become absolutely still, lost completely in her own mind, shocked that she had just blurted that out without any coaxing. If she only knew!

Dan looked at her sharply. "When do you do that?"

"While you sleep," she said, never looking over at him, avoiding eye contact.

"Why?"

"I like to look for other fires, listen for voices. I like to think there's still hope for us yet."

"After everything you put yourself through?" he said ignorantly. "Why didn't you tell me any of this?"

"I don't know."

"What the hell, Kenndra? Well now I know why you're always so tired. Is that why we stopped exercising?"

"You can exercise anytime you want. Don't yell at me, okay? There's no point in yelling."

"Unbelievable." Dan crossed his arms.

Kenndra looked at her nails stained a faint green, the two of them alone in total silence save for the fire crackling next to them, neither doing anything but breathe, watching the orange and yellow flames flittering and snapping upward against the black background.

"I saw something last time," she said after a while. Her admission had the weight of a deathbed confession, another sign of the end encroaching on them if they were aware enough to pick up on it. It was an announcement so out-of-character for her that she couldn't bring herself to make eye contact with him after she said it, overcome with the shame of a secret kept too long. Dan looked at her, angry that she would keep something like that from him for even a moment, but even more so because of the jarring implications of seeing something other than infinite darkness. *She was talking about me of course. She saw* me.

"Do you remember when we were in our apartment together, right before all this? We were arguing about the cable and you were drinking beer on the porch with your back to me. I came up in the doorway behind you to say that I was leaving for good, but before I could, something caught my eye. Out in the distance, across the parking lot, there was a man in a brown suit and red bowtie staring at the two of us, and he was standing under the shade of those big trees. Do you remember that?"

Dan nodded, anxious for her to get to the point.

"I saw him again," she said. "It was like he was standing behind a black curtain, like all this darkness around us can just be pushed aside, and he leaned out to look at me—at us. I could only see his face and shoulders, but I'm sure it was him except this time his face was white and his nose was bright red. Like a clown, kind of."

"How long was he looking at you?"

"Only a few seconds."

"Then what?"

"He waved at me and went back behind the curtain again. I sat there for a long time after that waiting for him to appear again, but he never did. I thought we were saved, Dan. I thought it was about to be over for us here."

"We have to find out who he is," said Dan, intrigued, forgetting his anger. "He'll come back, and when he does we'll get his attention, " and so for the first time in a long time they both agreed to climb to the top of the mound together to wait for me.

From behind my curtain, I listened to them talk for a while and based on their tones of voice and sudden bursts of laughter, it was apparent that their relationship had been reinvigorated by their new mission to spot me, a sudden opportunity to bond again after what seemed to both of them, in their own private ways, a vast amount of time drifting apart. Over time, they had become individuals right next to each other, morphed into nothing more than familiar strangers, stuck together between the fire and the mound for so, so long. Now they made plans, looked to the future, but truth be told it was nothing more than a game I was playing with myself now. It would be hide-and-seek right up until the end.

"What should we do if he peeks in again?" asked Kenndra.

"We'll go after him if we have to," said Dan. "Maybe he can help get us out of here," and so down on the page, sitting on top of the mound, I left Dan and Kenndra alone again, waiting for me to reveal myself to them, explain everything, but of course I never would.

Kennardo Goes to the Racetrack

I had seen him before the race started, standing in line at the gate with a literal sack of money, like a pillowcase bag with a black money symbol painted on it, which he hauled up onto the counter and pushed towards the teller who just looked at him and the bag like, What the fuck is this? then I overheard him say he wanted all of it on The Big Canard to win.

After The Big Canard finished in a distant last place, on my way out later, after a few more races, I remember seeing him lying on a bench outside the entrance, staring up into the sky with his arms crossed over his chest, dejected and sad, his white face paint smeared a bit around his eyes like he had been crying, his big red shoes sticking straight up, higher than the back of the bench, and he had somehow already made a sign on a scrap of cardboard that said, "Lost everything, please help," with his crumpled brown hat sitting upside down on the ground in front of it.

Kennardo Visits Kenndra

I'll never forget it because it was right after Dan and I had a big argument about where our relationship was going, and how he was approaching his job lately, and how it was making me feel, and I was still very emotional about it all. Should we break up, should we not? Neither of us knew what to do. Anyway, I remember I had stayed pretty late at work that day to get a few extra things done and to avoid going home just yet, and I was sitting behind my desk thinking about Dan, scrutinizing the idea of whether or not he could be the One after all of the things we argued about, which opened up a real can of worms. I was thinking about what my mother would say about him, about what I was doing with my life, considering whether or not I could bring myself to start all over again with someone else, having all these thoughts, when in walks this hobo clown.

He was wearing a rumpled brown suit that was too big for him, a plastic flower pinned to his lapel, and he had a white face and red puffball nose with a thick brown beard like Dan used to have. I remember feeling nervous right away, like what the fuck is this person doing in my office? But he just stood there inside the doorway silently surveying the room, glancing from the stacks of cardboard boxes I still needed to unpack to the boring, undecorated gray walls to the slanted blinds in the windows. My office was a mess, I realized, but it also struck me in that moment watching him examine my office that I had never brought in a picture of Dan to put on my desk after all the time we had been together.

"Can I help you with something?" I asked.

I was staring at him, and I began to think he looked familiar, like maybe he could have been Dan in clown makeup, which was a delightful thought for me at the time—to think of him dressed like a clown. Maybe it was his new job.

"Dan, is that you?"

I blinked and he was standing on the other side of my desk—then I remember feeling confused and disoriented, wondering how he got so close to me without ever seeing him move. He fumbled through his jacket, putting on an act for me, turning all of his pockets inside out, emptying hard candies and rubber bands and pencil erasers and bits of string and confetti onto the floor.

"Who are you?" I asked. "What are you doing?"

He sat down on the edge of my desk, so close that I could smell him, and I was compelled to close my eyes and breathe him in, thinking he smelled like trampled flowers and rainwater, a combination that for some reason conjured up memories of my childhood, and thinking of my childhood I remembered an old picture of myself from when I was seven. It was on my mother's nightstand for years, one of her favorite pictures of me. I was standing in a recreation league soccer uniform, purple jersey and tall white socks with purple stripes, the short white shorts, my hair pulled back in a ponytail, the green field stretching behind me, one foot up on the ball. It was the picture I had of myself in my mind whenever I thought of myself as ever having been a little girl, back when the rest of my life had yet to happen.

I opened my eyes again and he was offering me a white handkerchief, so I reached out to take it from him, to wipe a tear from the corner of my eye—but the white handkerchief was tied to a blue one inside his jacket, and the blue one to a purple one, and the purple one to a green one, and the green one to a red one, and the red one to an orange one, and the orange one to a yellow one, and his expression the whole time was one of utter shock and surprise, as if he had no idea how all those handkerchiefs got tied together and put into his coat pocket.

I continued to pull more and more handkerchiefs to the point I had gathered a large pile in my lap, and I wondered how many more there could possibly be. As I was pulling, he was backpedaling his way out of my office as he continued to unravel an impossible number of handkerchiefs from inside his jacket. He paused in the doorframe—grinning, making me grin with him, and for a moment everything seemed okay again. He removed his hat and bowed and then backed out fully into the hallway. When my body finally caught up to what I was seeing in my brain, I threw the pile of handkerchiefs off my lap and rushed for the door.

"Wait a second!" I yelled.

I gripped the doorframe and leaned out into the hallway to try and catch him, to tell him something, but it was like he had jumped from a plane—he was gone. Looking up and down the empty hallway, everything went slipping away from me all at once as if it were just a dream, but it wasn't. It was real. As real as you and me right now.

The Revelation of an Unsettling
Truth

It was Friday afternoon, and it became clear that once my colleagues realized Ken was only interested in talking about Kennard, they quickly lost patience with him. Their expressions made it painfully obvious to anyone with a sense for body language that they were anxious for this meeting to end, especially because it had nothing to do with the usual business.

I looked at everyone around the table: Scott was picking at his fingernails, Diane was glaring at her watch obnoxiously, no doubt fretting about her dropping Efficiency Ratios, thinking about what other, more productive things she could be doing at the moment instead of being in this conference room with Ken. Kennard was a new hire set to start on Monday and the unlikely subject of this meeting. Then there was me, Gary, acting as witness to it all.

"I need to know if any of you know anything about

him," pleaded Ken. "It's important."

"Why?" said Scott, dropping a tiny worm of dirt to the floor next to him.

"Because I'm developing a theory regarding my relationship with Kennard—all of our relationships with Kennard" said Ken. "I know how that sounds, but—"

"—Don't bring me into this," blurted Diane. "He means nothing to me. I've never met him."

"Diane, first of all, come on, you're already involved. Trust me. We all are. This is just the beginning. I think you'll see that it's quite incredible when you understand what I'm getting at here. I have proof," said Ken. "He's been leaving me notes. Now granted, if I'm understanding his notes so far you're all just side characters, so perhaps that's why you don't care as much as I do, but—"

"Wait. Who's been leaving you notes?" said Scott.

"Kennard," said Ken, frustrated with Scott and Diane's denseness. Callousness, really.

"The guy who starts next week?" In tone and expression, Scott was both annoyed and dumbfounded, and making it quite clear that he regarded this meeting as an utter waste of his time. He looked around the conference room like he wasn't sure where he was anymore, like he had appeared there against his will, possibly wondering how in the hell his life ended up the way it did. According to Ken's burgeoning theory of reality, it was because of Kennard—for me and for everyone else sitting around the table impatiently. "What the fuck is going on with you?" he hissed, his eyes narrowing. "I'm offended by all of this."

"No one knows what you're talking about, Ken," snapped Diane, chewing her gum with an open mouth.

"I had a feeling you would all react this way. I wouldn't

believe me either if I were you. I hardly believe it myself, but put yourself in *my position* for a minute. It's been days now of these notes appearing—on my desk, on the front door of my house, on the fucking steering wheel of my car. Are one of you playing a joke on me? Because if you are, now would be the time to tell me."

"No one has time for that," said Diane. "I mean, *seriously.*"

"That *is* pretty weird, though," I admitted. "Where are they coming from?"

"Thanks, Gary, I appreciate that," said Ken. "That's exactly what I'm trying to figure out."

"I don't know why he's leaving you notes, but that's between you and him," said Diane.

"I've never met the man or spoken to the man, I don't know anything about him, and I'd like to return to my cubicle now," said Scott.

"Me too," said Diane. "I second all of that."

"Wait a second," I said. "I want to see the notes. Do you have them?"

"Of course." Ken pulled a folded wad of notebook papers from inside his sportcoat and tossed them confidently into the center of the table. "There they are."

"I want to bash my head in listening to this," said Scott.

"Read them, Gary," insisted Ken. "I need to know what you think."

"I think you need to be talking to HR about this, not us," said Scott. "Dude sounds like a creeper to me."

"What about you, Gary?" he said.

Knowing Ken like I had for so many years, I felt like I had to humor him a bit even if it felt impossible to believe what he was saying. I read the first note and it said, "Hey Ken, guess what? You're a character in my story, your life is not a real life the way you think it is, and everything you do and everything you say and everyone you've ever met are a fabrication of my mind. You are nothing more than a collection of my sentences! Hahahaha!" and it was signed at the bottom, "Dan Kennard."

Even though no one believed that the notes could possibly be true, they were menacing in their way, and I shuddered briefly at the thought of not being real. If someone *was* playing a joke on him, it was a dark one. I could tell already that he was beginning to question his understanding of his whole life, and he was either going off the deep end or they really were characters in a story together. That no one showed even the slightest concern about either predicament made it even more of a horror.

"Are we done here?" asked Diane. "My Efficiency Ratios and Screen Time numbers have dipped with me being sick and all last month, so I can't afford to keep sitting here. I gots to go."

"I second that," said Scott. "Talk to HR. I'm out of here. Happy Friday everybody."

As Scott and Diane shuffled out of the conference room, I read the note he had numbered two. It said: "Starting Monday, I will prove it to you!" with a little hand drawn picture of a duck in sunglasses next to his name this time. The third one said, "Enjoy your last weekend!" with the same little cartoon duck drawn in the bottom corner. I folded them up and handed them back to Ken.

"I think Scott is right, you should talk to HR about it and maybe they could do something."

"Come on, Gary," he replied. "You know me the best here. I'm not crazy, am I?"

"No, Ken. You're not crazy." I tried to avert my eyes

from his, but the intensity of his stare held mine for a moment longer, long enough to consider taking him more seriously than anyone else ever would. He needed affirmation of some kind.

"How is he getting into our building, Gary? How does he know where I live? These notes are really fucking with my mind."

"I don't know, Ken." It was pathetic, but it was all I could think to say. As we both prepared to leave, we stood across from each other in silence for a few moments.

"I just don't know why he would pick *me*. I don't want to be a protagonist. Isn't that the one who all the shit happens to?"

"Look at it this way. After all the shit, they're also the one who gets the big prize at the end too. Maybe this will be good for you." I laughed because I didn't know what else to do. I clapped him on the back in the most friendly, supportive way that I could. I tried to send a lot of optimistic messages through that back-clap, and then we went back to our desks to finish out the day.

That was Friday afternoon, but, sure enough, in less than a week's time everything that went on to happen to Ken— the sudden ubiquity of the ducks, the odd suffering we were forced to bear witness to as the beard consumed him—it all seemed to circle back to Kennard somehow.

Lemming, our supervisor, had sent an email the week before informing us that there would be a new addition to our office pod, a guy named Dan Kennard, and that he would be starting on Monday. He insisted that we should all be welcoming and friendly, and so on, show him the ropes, but when he first arrived that morning, suddenly appearing in our office pod doorway seemingly out of nowhere, the first thing I remembered thinking when I saw him was, "Holy shit, that guy looks just like Ken." It was jarring.

I remember he paused in the doorway, looking in at us as if he was searching the room for someone before Lemming came up happily behind him and escorted him to Office Nook 33, which had been specially prepared over the weekend for his arrival. Ken was already in the office at the time, having arrived before all of us as usual, working away in his big green headphones like he used to do while Lemming explained some last minute details of the job to Dan.

I glanced over at Ken a couple of nooks down from me to see if he noticed the arrival of his apparent antagonist, and also to confirm for myself that the two men were not one and the same. Sure enough, Ken was clacking away at his keyboard, oblivious at the moment to the fact that his doppelgänger had just walked in and taken the nook immediately behind him. I stood from my desk chair and went over to introduce myself to Dan the same way I would have for any new hire.

"Welcome to Klyber, Mr. Kennard. I'm Gary." We shook hands.

"Gary is a good man," said Lemming, slapping me on the shoulder. "He's been here so long, you can ask him anything and he'll know the answer. Right, Gary?"

"Right," I said flatly.

"Gary could probably do my job," said Lemming. "Anyway, Mr. Kennard, if you don't have any more questions for me, you can ask Gary anything. Show him the ropes, Gary, you know what I mean." He winked at me. "Um, coffee is in the break room down the hallway, help yourself if you're into that, and I'll check back in a little later to see how things are going."

As Lemming walked away I said, "Welcome to Klyber, Dan."

"Thanks," he said. "Who's that?" He pointed at Ken, still going right next to me.

"That's Ken Dannerd. He's a good man. Been here practically as long as I have." We were the only three people in our pod at the moment. "He's not a big talker. He's a worker, and that's the kind of people we like around here," I went on, feeling an awkward tinge of duty to set some abstract standard of performance, but when he didn't bother replying we both ended up just sort of staring at each other.

After a few moments of silence, I couldn't help myself—I had to say something. I was thinking of Ken the whole time I was looking at Dan, feeling shook by the uncanny resemblance—the side-parted hair cut, the gray glasses and dark eyebrows, the clean-shaven face and the slight gap in his front teeth—and even though it was probably an awkward way to continue a conversation, I finally said, "You know...I have to say, work stuff aside, you look an awful lot like Ken."

I stepped to the side as if I were presenting Ken as a gift for him to see and assess for himself, but he only grinned at me condescendingly, like it was a joke he'd heard before, like he already knew he looked like Ken, and then he said with what I could only interpret as complete indifference, "I don't know. Maybe."

I looked back at Ken still typing away at his desk, suddenly unsure of myself, feeling because of his grin like I was being messed with somehow, and I became more awkward than I've ever been. He was already having an oddly powerful effect over how I carried myself, and I found myself back-tracking a bit. "Well, you may be right. Ken doesn't have a beard like you."

"Not yet," he replied.

I didn't know what that meant at the time, but I cleared

my throat and reached out to put my hand firmly on Ken's shoulder, deciding in the moment that I should introduce the two of them and Ken spun around in his chair and looked up at me with surprise, accustomed as he was to not being interrupted while he had his headphones on.

When he saw Dan standing there he froze for a moment, looking up at him from his chair with fear and awe. Even then, you could see in the sudden uncertainty of his body as he rose nervously from his desk chair that he felt something powerful seizing upon him, no doubt thinking of the notes.

"Ken, this is Dan," I said. "Dan...this is Ken."

They looked at each other, straight into the eyes, a long stare-down ensuing as they each silently regarded the other until Ken put his hand out first and Dan raised his to meet it, and finally, briefly yet firmly, I watched them shake hands.

"I've been getting your messages," said Ken.

"Oh good, I like to introduce myself early," said Dan, "so people can get a sense of who I am."

"A fucking weirdo?" said Ken. "Because that's the sense I got with these damn notes. You didn't leave anyone else any notes, did you?"

"I didn't need to. I'll be working most closely with you."

They continued to stare at each other for a few more moments, neither of them willing to say anymore until Ken finally said, "Well, I look forward to that, but if you'll excuse me, I'm going to get back to work over here. Lots to do, lots to type up," and he turned and sat down again, taking a moment to position his headphones over his ears.

"So I suppose that's your desk behind you there?" I asked, peeking over Dan's shoulder and finding that it was mostly empty except for a small yellow rubber duck he had somehow already managed to set up underneath his computer monitor and which happened to be angled directly towards me. I felt the strange sensation of making eye contact with it. "Anyway, like Lemming said, if you have any questions about anything feel free to ask one of us. We're a friendly bunch," and then I went back to my nook and sat down again.

I tried to settle into my work for the day, but as I took a few sips from my coffee, now lukewarm, I couldn't bring myself to do anything else at first except stare back and forth between them. For much of the day after that, I couldn't help but compare them, searching for their various points of sameness, which I would find included everything from their posture to the way they walked around the office; even their voices were nearly identical so that if I weren't looking at them I wouldn't be able to tell which one was speaking. And to top it all off, because their nooks were back-to-back, from my vantage point a few nooks down it was like watching someone work in front of a wall-sized mirror, except that Dan had a beard and Ken didn't—at least not yet.

It was probably around eight-thirty in the morning on Kennard's second day when Ken came into the break room, patting his forehead with a folded napkin. I was leaning against the counter making another cup of coffee, placing the coffee pod into the machine when he walked in. He was rubbing under his eyes, looking exasperated and tired. I watched him for a few seconds before I said, "Hey Ken, are you okay?"

'I'm fine,' he said, but he only made glancing eye contact with me, nervous, like he was hiding something, the revelation of something profound glowing from his face. He went over to the sink and washed his hands with his back to me. I watched him splash water on his face and then dry it with a paper towel before he turned to me again. "I was having a hard time concentrating at my desk," he said finally.

"You should eat something," I said. That was something my mother would have told me. I was trying to be helpful and I couldn't think of anything else to say, neither of us totally sure of what might be happening. Behind me, the coffee machine hissed and began to spit coffee into my cup.

"I had some bread earlier."

"What are you...a duck?" I joked. "You should eat something else too. Man can't live on bread alone. Drink some water too. Water is good for everything."

It was hard to tell if he was listening because his face was angled down at the space in front of his shoes, the wet paper towel in his fist dripping water onto the checkered linoleum floor of our break room. Then he said, "It's hard to explain, Gary. It feels like the floor is slanted against me or something."

I didn't know what to say to that. I tried to picture it for a moment in my mind, to empathize, but I couldn't. It felt like there was glass between us ever since Dan arrived the day before. "Did you talk to HR?"

"No."

"Why not? That would have been the first thing I would have done."

"What good would it do, Gary? If I'm just a character in some story and he's the author, he can do whatever he wants with me—with any of us. You too, you know."

"I'm just a side character, Ken, you said it yourself." I was trying to make a joke, but he didn't laugh. "Maybe you're getting sick," I said. "Maybe these are the early signs of something."

You have to understand that when I said all of this, I was only making conversation. I was being polite in my helplessness; it doesn't mean that I knew anything. I didn't want to be right.

It's always hard to decide when to step in and involve yourself or stay out of things and mind your own business, but whatever it was that Dan was doing to Ken, it became visible quickly. The next day, Wednesday, I felt like I had no choice but to step in, so when I thought I ran into Ken in the men's room, I decided to strike up a more direct conversation. We were standing next to each other at the urinals and I said, "Hey, man, are you feeling any better?"

Both of us were staring at the walls in front of us, the sound of our urine tinkling into the ceramic bowls, rising to crescendo. "Me? Sure, I'm fine. Why, do I look sick?" We turned our heads and made brief eye contact.

"Well, ever since yesterday I've been wondering how you're doing. You didn't seem so good when we talked."

We flushed the toilets and zipped our pants, turning at the same time to head over to the sinks to wash our hands. We were standing side-by-side again when I said, "If you don't want to talk to HR, I think you need to confront Kennard about the notes, straight up."

I'll never forget his response: without breaking eye contact with himself in the mirror—just looking straight into his own eyes, into his own reflection—he held his hands under the running water and said, "But I *am* Kennard."

I could feel the blood rushing to my face in embarrassment. "So you shaved, huh? I'm sorry. I thought you were Ken this whole time." I didn't know what else to say. I pumped some foamy soap into my palm and rubbed my hands together under the faucet. Of course, I should have paid closer attention, and now that it was out in the open it seemed to become obvious all of a sudden. It was that grin of his. I never knew what to make of it.

"Besides, Ken isn't at work today," he added. "He called out sick." He yanked a paper towel from the dispenser and dried his hands with it, but I was made frozen at the sink because as long as I've been at Klyber and as long as I've known Ken, he's never once called out sick.

That afternoon sitting at the lunch table with Scott and Diane, I said, "Did you two notice that Ken is out sick today?"

"Yeah, so?" said Scott.

"Yeah so?" I replied in disbelief. "Ken hasn't called out sick in years."

"I guess I didn't notice," said Scott.

"What are you getting at?" said Diane. "You think this has something to do with the notes?"

"What if he's right? What if this is just Kennard making him sick?"

"How would Kennard be making Ken sick?" said Scott.

"Well…I don't know, but there's something going on there. I don't trust him."

"What do you mean?" said Diane.

"I don't know. The notes he shared with us, for one thing. I'm starting to believe him. They look the same too, right? Am I the only one who thinks they look the same? Kennard shaved his beard today and I was talking to him earlier thinking he was Ken." I looked at the rest of them around the table for looks of confirmation.

"But what does that have to do with anything?" said Scott.

"I don't know. Strikes me as odd. Kennard shows up and then Ken gets sick for the first time ever. You tell me what it means."

"Coincidence," said Scott. "That's all it is."

I took a bite of my peanut butter and jelly sandwich, chewed a bit, swallowed, and then said, "No, no. There's something going on. I can feel it. What about their names? Is that coincidence too? I feel like Kennard is here to replace Ken somehow."

None of them had thought about their names, the layers of potential meaning, the implication that there was some kind of metaphysical cosmic connection between the two of them, that perhaps the notes *were* true. I don't want to toot my own horn because I wish I was wrong about it all, but it was clear I had taken Ken the most seriously out of all of us.

"Should we call him?" suggested Diane.

"Call Ken?"

"Yeah, call him up and ask him."

"I suppose." I slid my cell phone from my pocket and looked at it. "I'm nervous."

"Why?"

"I don't know."

"Call him," they said. "Ask him how he's doing."

They all sat around the table, watched me dial, and then put the phone to my ear. "It's ringing," I said. I plugged my open ear with a finger and I took another bite of my sandwich, sending a glob of red jelly falling onto the table. "Ken? It's Gary," I said, swallowing quickly, looking at the rest of them. They leaned in to hear us better, and a hush came over them as they listened to Ken's voice on the other end of the phone, tiny and distant. "How's it going, man?" I tried to give the table updates as he explained himself, covering my phone with a hand. "He says he's on his way back from the doctor's office right now." Speaking back into the phone again I said, "So what did the doctor say?" I listened intently. "Well that's good I guess; at least it's not getting any worse, right? How are you feeling today? Uh-huh. Quakcuetarol? I've never heard of that." I made a face at the others to see if they had heard of it, but they all just shrugged. "I was calling because we're all in the break room eating lunch and talking about you. We were just saying how we aren't used to having an empty seat next to us." I laughed nervously and looked around the table at everyone else to gauge their expressions. "Anyway, I just wanted to check in, man. When are you coming back? Uh-huh. Well good, we'll see you tomorrow then, rest up buddy," and then I hung up.

"You didn't ask him about Dan," said Scott as soon as I slipped the phone back into my pocket. "Wasn't that the whole reason you called?"

"The doctor gave him some medicine, so I figured I didn't need to ask. He said he's feeling way better."

They were all looking at me over the table disappointed when in walked Kennard with his own lunch. "Mind if I sit down with you guys?" he asked.

Of course we said yes, that we didn't mind at all. We welcomed him to the table, and then we all watched as Dan went and sat down in Ken's seat.

Ken came back the next day just like I said he would, but it was like he was drunk or something. I asked him if he was feeling any better, but Ken couldn't stop talking about these ducks that he said were waiting for him on his front steps when he came home from the doctor's office. He said there was a group of them waiting at his front door like they were expecting to be let in, like they lived there with him or something.

"So they were real?" I said. I immediately found myself thinking of the drawings of ducks on the notes and found my heart pounding.

"I had to use my feet to block them from coming in!" said Ken, bewildered. "They were there this morning too, huddled in the driveway behind my car just quacking away. I think I backed over one of them on the way out. Damn things wouldn't get out of the way!" He let out a sigh and slouched into his desk chair.

"Maybe you should go back to the doctor again. I say that as a friend."

"I should call the county is what I should do—have them come take the damn things away." He rubbed his eyes wearily.

Kennard, who was behind him typing the whole time, must have been listening because he turned around in his desk chair to face Ken and said, "Did any of them happen to be wearing red bow-ties?"

"What the fuck kind of question is that?" I said, glaring at Kennard defensively.

Ken spun around in his chair as if he was just waiting for Dan to say something so he could finally confront him, and for the first time since they met, they were face-to-face with each other. "Wait a second, Gary." Ken wheeled his desk chair a little closer to Kennard and leaned forward. "Why would any of them be wearing red bow-ties?" he asked, seething in a way that suggested if Dan gave a certain kind of answer Ken might try to kill him.

"Because ducks don't wear bow-ties," said Kennard. "Unless you live in a story. Then anything is possible."

Ken's face flushed red and he took a long look at Kennard, staring him right in the eyes, his jaw clenched. "What do you know about it!" he exploded, standing from his chair. "You fucking freak!" and before I could stop him, Ken kicked

Dan's chair and sent him wheeling back against his desk. "What are you doing to me!" he shouted.

"Ken, stop!" I said, grabbing him from behind and pulling him back. "Cool it, man. Cool it." Ken was breathing through his teeth and glaring at Dan, who met his eyes with a steady, smirky gaze, unblinking, looking up at him calmly from his desk chair. "Let's go take a walk," I said, pulling Ken back by the shoulders, breaking the powerful magnetism between the two. "Let's go get some air, come on."

Right after that, as if triggered by the escalation, the beard started.

Ken wasn't usually a smoker, but once we got outside I offered him one from my pack anyway and he took it without hesitation. We stood in the sun smoking silently for a few minutes, looking out at the parking lot that seemed to stretch off to the horizon, the gray silhouette of the Sunset City skyscrapers visible through the mid-day haze. It was the first time I had ever considered that the skyline might simply be painted on.

Ken was preoccupied and distant, and standing next to him he suddenly felt smaller and shorter than I remembered, his clothes growing baggy on his body like he was shrinking inside them, already on his way out of our world, whatever it was.

"The ducks had red bow-ties on," he admitted. He took a long drag on his cigarette and blew the smoke into the sky where it swirled and dispersed. "He's from another world, Gary. We're his playthings. We're his little toys. He was telling the truth in those notes. I stood there looking at them in my driveway thinking: This can't be real. I'm dreaming. I'm still sleeping, but I knew it was him sending them because of the pictures on his notes. It was terrifying, to realize in a single moment that everything you thought you knew was a lie, to realize that your life isn't yours and never was."

I was speechless.

He flicked his cigarette into the parking lot where the morning sun glared brightly, sharply off the cars. In the distance was the vague woosh of traffic going by. I dropped my cigarette stub to the ground and smothered it with my shoe.

"He was in one of my dreams last night. I was in a shoebox, real tiny, and he was peeking inside—like I was a bug he had captured or something. I can barely think straight right now. I feel weak."

"You don't look so good either, I have to say. You should go home. Take the rest of the day off. That's what I'd do. You never take days off anyway, you probably have a million days to use."

"What if the ducks are still there?" he asked seriously.

"Then run them over with your damn car," I said laughing, expecting Ken to laugh too, trying to lighten the mood, but he just squinted out into the glare of the parking lot. The sun was hitting his face in such a way that I could see the stubble on his cheeks and chin, and in the few seconds I was looking at him before we went back inside, I swear I saw it growing before my eyes, as subtle as the moving hands of a clock.

Once Lemming heard that Ken had threatened Kennard, or vice-versa, he called them both into his office to straighten everything out. Kennard returned first and we all watched Ken come staggering behind him at a slight distance, swimming in his clothes by then and his beard suddenly thick enough to grab with your fingertips and pull on.

By that point it was impossible to deny his beard was growing right before our eyes, and he passed by us with his eyes down like a prisoner on his way to the gallows, which in hindsight is precisely what he was ever since the notes began to appear. Even Scott and Diane believed him now, the shock and awe evident by their gaped mouths and the tightened brows of their faces. Ken collapsed into his desk chair, Kennard already in his behind him, shuffling through some papers on his desk acting innocent.

"Hey, Ken," I said. "You need to go home, man. You need to see the doctor again."

"I second that," said Scott. "I can see your beard growing as we speak."

Ken turned and looked at me like he wasn't sure who I was, and I remember thinking he had the look in his eyes of someone who was very deep inside their own mind. In the few moments between emerging from Lemming's office and sitting in his chair, we had all watched his beard grow passed his shirt collar. He didn't say anything to either of us, but simply stared.

"Ken? Did you hear me?" I asked, and when he didn't respond again I said, "I'm calling you an ambulance." I took out my phone and dialed 9-1-1. "Hi, we have an emergency over here at Klyber Corp. We need an ambulance right away," and I recited the address to the dispatcher.

By then, Ken's beard was growing faster than ever, the hair emerging like paper through the bottom of a shredder from his face until Ken's sideburns and mustache and beard and eyebrows and hair—all of it—engulfed his head, curling up over his nose and eyes and forehead until soon enough his face was completely masked from view. Beneath it all I could hear him muttering, "This isn't real, this isn't real, this isn't real," over and over again.

I grabbed a set of scissors from my desk and began cutting off huge chunks of hair from over his face as he continued to mutter from beneath it all, but Ken's hair was growing faster than I could cut it off until soon enough his beard had expanded beyond his face and engulfed him in his chair, draped over his shoulders and down his chest, flowing from his body like foam from a dishwasher and before we knew it, it was cascading down the back of his desk chair until eventually it was touching the floor on all sides of him and he completely disappeared from our sight, concealed by a blanket of curly brown hair.

We gathered around him and Diane started praying through her tears for it to stop, her concern coming much too late, but none of us could look away. He continued to mutter "this isn't real, this isn't real," his voice weakening with each repetition until he was finally rendered silent.

After a few moments, I called out to him. "Ken? Are you still there?"

We stood around him stunned until Scott said, "I think it stopped growing," and everyone except for Kennard, who already knew the ending, leaned in closer to see.

Outside we could hear the Sunset City ambulance sirens growing louder as they approached our building, but by the time the pair of EMTs came rushing into our cubicle-area, the only thing left of Ken was a mound of coarse brown hair. Nothing of his body was visible anymore other than the wheels of his desk chair and the tips of his shoes poking out from underneath.

As the EMTs approached, the rest of us backed away to give them space, but we already knew it was too late. One of them turned to us and said, "What the fuck is this? What happened in here?" No one spoke. No one knew what to say.

The medic turned back to the pile of hair and began to search through it, parting the hair with his latex-gloved hands, nervous, like something might reach out and grab him. When he was elbow-deep into the mound of hair, he turned to us with a look of surprise. "Wait a second," he said. "I think I feel something."

He grabbed the mound of hair and shifted it to the ground next to the chair revealing Ken's evacuated suit underneath, left behind like an empty shell, and his body somehow replaced by a tiny yellow duckling nestled in the collar of his shirt.

As the medic lifted the duckling from the pile of hair to show us, Diane gasped and covered her mouth and Scott stood as if he were hypnotized by the whole event, hands in his pockets. To me it felt like the conclusion of a magic trick, like any minute I was supposed to start clapping and out would walk Ken, perfectly fine. It had to be a joke. We would all find out the medic was in on it too somehow, that it was all just a prank set up between Ken and Kennard and we'd all end up back-slapping our way out to happy hour, but that's not what happened. I looked around for Kennard, but he was no longer there either, Ken and Dan disappearing together in the same instant.

After the police arrived, and while the fire fighters searched the rest of the building for either of them, I remember standing at my desk, unable to concentrate on anything, milling around with Lemming and the rest of them, all of us waiting to give our statements about what we knew. In the end, though, I'll never forget the image of the two medics kneeling down next to Ken's desk chair, one holding the duckling in his cupped hands, unsure what to do with it, while the other, kneeling next to him, began stuffing the hair and the empty suit into a big black evidence bag knowing we would never see either one of them again.

Kennardo Goes Out for a Drink

I was bartending at the Quack House at the time, and it was a slow night, an odd night in retrospect, so slow that it actually began to feel like something was happening that I wasn't in on. Like maybe the rest of the city was burning to the ground and no one had bothered to tell me about the evacuation. The bar-area was completely empty, which never happens, and I remember I was drying pint glasses with a towel when he just appeared out of thin air. I didn't even hear the door open or catch him in a reflection or hear a footstep creak the old Quack House floors, he just appeared in mid-stride almost, mid-movement, like he had stepped through a portal from another dimension and into the bar.

I didn't know who he was, I just thought he was some fucked up dude in clown makeup. He sat down at the bar and looked around, looking at the bottles of liquor behind me, the row of beer taps.

"Hey there," I said. "What's the occasion?"

"What occasion?"

"You coming from a party?"

"What party?"

"That's what I'm asking you." I tried to make eye contact with him because I thought maybe he was already drunk, the way he was talking and all, but it was hard to tell. He would look at me briefly, but never in the eyes, always at the space between my eyebrows or the tip of my ear, and I couldn't get a read on him at all.

"How about a drink first. Then I'll answer all your questions."

"Okay, what can I get you?"

He raised his eyebrows. "Are there any specials going on?"

"Dollar off well cocktails, dollar off draft beers."

"I'll take a scotch and soda with ice."

I made his drink and put it down in front of him. He stirred it glumly with the tip of a finger, the ice clinking against the glass as it swirled.

"So you coming from somewhere?" I asked.

"What is that supposed to mean?" he said, looking over my shoulder now.

"You're dressed like a clown."

"I know."

"So where are you coming from?"

"Why would I be coming from anywhere?"

"Because you're dressed like a clown."

"I *am* a clown. This is who I am."

"So you dress like a clown to go out to a bar?"

"I'm not sure what you're trying to get at. You're a bartender and I'm a clown. Why do you wear that tight black shirt with the duck logo on it?"

"Quack House uniform."

"Well there you go. There's your answer."

"How can you drink with that nose on your nose?"

"I use my mouth."

"Does your flower squirt water?"

"Sure." He demonstrated by squirting some water into his drink.

"What else can you do?"

"Almost anything I want."

"Prove it," I said, and for the first time since he sat down he looked me square in the eyes, snapped a finger above his head and fucking disappeared off his barstool. The only thing left was his drink, empty except for the ice and his red, puff-ball nose on top.

Birdsong

The thing that most people don't fully understand is that I shudder at the thought of my life being any different now. As traumatizing as it was for the people in the room to witness, for me it was like snatching a new life from the ashes of an old, dying one. But it never would have happened without everything going the way it did, without Kennard breathing down my neck at every turn. Kennard is the real hero here, because without him pushing me towards my destiny, I would have never become the person I am now: a man of peace and tranquility, a man at ease with the world, monastic. So despite the fact that I can no longer talk or smell, and I have so many headaches and memory problems, I can honestly say that it was all for the better.

   It started when Kennard—who is my boss and a man I try desperately to avoid at all times—comes up to me on Friday afternoon right as I was about to walk out the door and go home for the weekend. I'm about to push the door open when he cuts me off from out of nowhere, stepping in front of me out of a side hallway where he had apparently been waiting, and he launches into this tirade, somehow sensing that I planned on skipping Required Training.

He said, "You better be at Required Training tomorrow morning or it's your life. We know you. We keep track of everything around here, we're data-driven, and we know what you're thinking and we say don't even think about it, or you won't be working here anymore. You'll have nothing, you Fuckstick."

He grilled me with his eyes as he spoke, getting close enough to my face that I could feel the heat of his breath as he poked me in the center of my chest with his finger to reiterate his seriousness, foaming in the corners of his mouth, his forehead red hot.

When I got home, I told my girlfriend everything he said to me and about how he called me a Fuckstick right to my face and about the foamy spittle.

"Isn't it illegal to talk to me that way?"

"What, are we going to bring a lawsuit up now?"

"If we can, why not?"

"He sounds smart to me," she said. "He explicitly told you to attend or you would lose your job, so if you skipped it now you'd only end up proving him right. Is that what you want?"

I twisted the top off of a beer bottle and looked at her. "He's the Fuckstick," I said.

"You have to go. You have no choice now. He wins." She looked me straight in the eyes.

"But I've done this training already. It's too much. It's a farce! I don't think I can do it again. It's the same thing over and over. I can't take it anymore. Plus, on top of that, it's a Saturday. How many days a week can they take from us?"

"Maybe you'll pass it this time," she snarked.

"I don't know how I haven't passed it already. I don't even know what the requirements are for passing. We fold papers and answer meaningless hypothetical questions and we have shoulder partners we're supposed to discuss everything with—boxed sandwiches so we can work through lunch. It's horrendous." I took a long swig from my beer bottle.

"Have you asked anyone about why you're not passing?"

"I've sent emails."

"And?"

"And they don't reply."

"Are you talking to the correct people?"

"Kenndra, please. Don't pretend like I'm an idiot and don't know who to ask about these things. They just ignore me. I don't think they like me."

"Well, it's too late now anyway. You're trapped, Dan."

I swigged more from my beer and leaned on the counter, looking down at my shoes. She was right.

Early the next morning, I received a text message well before my alarm was set to go off that jolted me awake, a combination of the vibrating buzz and the glow of my screen lighting up the dark bedroom at the same time. I rolled over to look at it and turn the screen off, but then I saw it was from Kennard, so I swiped my finger across the screen to open the message.

My swipe revealed a tiny cartoon picture of an ax followed by an angry red emoji face and I defiantly pushed the button on the side of my phone to turn the screen off then dropped it back onto my nightstand before I rolled over into bed again to spoon with Kenndra for what would end up being the last time.

When I arrived at the Training Center later, it was as if the training had already been going on for hours. I took my usual seat near the window and happened to end up next to a colleague of mine whose name I can no longer remember, but I noticed that he had already taken over a page of notes so far.

"Where were you?" he whispered under his breath, adding something to his notes.

"What do you mean?"

"You're late. They took attendance. They were calling your name."

"How late am I?"

"Kennard was here looking for you earlier too. It started over an hour ago, we've already had a fifteen minute break."

"What? Really? And you've taken all those notes already?"

He nodded at me.

"Mind if I copy them down?"

I had only written down a few words when I felt my phone buzz inside my pocket. I took it out and placed it on the table next to my notepad, swiped my finger to see who it was. I saw that it was my boss again, sending me a picture of a clock and another angry-faced emoji. I showed my colleague the text message.

"Look at this," I said. "What is this?"

"He seems angry."

"He called me a Fuckstick yesterday, did you know that? Has he ever called you that?"

He shook his head at me.

"Can he call me that? Legally?"

He shrugged and kept his eyes on the front of the room, like I was bothering him, and I heard one of the two presenters ask the other for the location of the blue paper they intended to use for the next part of the training, but which they had apparently misplaced somehow.

"Do you think I should go up now or wait for the next break?"

"Why are you asking me?"

"What would you do if you were me?"

"I'd show up on time, first off."

"Haven't you done this before too?"

"No, but I want to pass the first time. I don't want to be like you."

"How do you pass?"

"Do you mind? I can't sit here and discuss all of this with you. I'm trying to understand what to do with this blue paper coming around." Apparently the blue paper had been located and one of the two presenters had begun walking around distributing it. He would be my shoulder partner for the rest of the day and I could already tell I was making him nervous.

Just then my phone started to buzz again, and I saw that it was Kenndra calling. I turned to my colleague and said, "I have to take this," and went out into the hallway.

In the hallway, just before the call went to voicemail, I swiped the screen to answer.

"Hello?"

"Dan, what is this letter?"

"What letter?"

"This letter I got in the mail today from Kennard. It says your pay has been docked."

"What? Does it say why?"

"He says you were late to your training today."

"But I'm here now."

"Well were you late? When did the training start?"

"I guess it started a little before I got here. Traffic was rough out there this morning—you know this city. How could you get a letter about it already though?"

"He must have anticipated your inevitable failure, Dan. He included a wallet photo of himself, too. He's cute."

"Don't say that."

"He's nothing like you described him."

"Please stop. That's my boss and we hate him, remember? We hate him as a collective unit because we're on the same team."

"Are you on a break right now?"

"No, you called me, so I excused myself. I figured it was an emergency."

"Good lord," she huffed. "You better not come home unless you pass this training. We can't afford this, Dan. We can't have you getting your pay docked."

"Well if you just texted me like a normal person, then I wouldn't have had to leave the room. Listen, I need to get back inside. They were passing out some blue paper and now I'm going to have no idea what to do with it. We'll talk about this later," I said and hung up the phone.

Back inside the training room, the lights had been turned off so that the presenters could show us a homemade video of their dogs playing, running freely around a vast backyard with perfect green grass, and I felt resentment swell in me at the fact that one of them had a backyard. I certainly didn't have a backyard—who could afford that? Not me. Not my wife and I combined. It was like they were showing off by playing the video. Dogs were expensive too, which I know because my wife and I had wanted a dog for years. Every time we saw them for adoption at the pet store we had to remind ourselves that we couldn't get one because we couldn't afford a house with a backyard because our jobs were so useless. We settled on a couple of fish instead. We could afford fish at least. I sat back down next to my colleague again and tried to concentrate on the training.

"What happened with the blue paper?" I asked.

"We're supposed to be folding it according to the movements of the dogs on screen. They say it says a lot about a person's acumen and intuitive knowledge based on how you fold it. They call it Interpretive Paper Folding."

"IPF. I remember that from before," I said confidently. "But we didn't use blue paper. We used some other color. Salmon, I think." I looked at the space in front of me and I didn't see any blue paper. "Where's my blue paper?" I asked. "Did they leave me a piece?"

I looked at him looking up at the video at the front of the room, then watched him fold his blue paper in half, then in half again, but diagonally, whatever the hell that meant. "How do I know?"

"You were sitting right here. You didn't tell them I was on the phone?"

"Was I supposed to?"

"I would have done that for you."

I watched him look from the video to his paper again, concentrating intensely before folding down a corner and turning the whole thing over, and I saw that he stuck his tongue out slightly whenever he was concentrating.

"I have an advanced degree," I pleaded, "and now I'm in a building somewhere folding paper to the movements of some aristocratic dogs! How about what my specialized degree says about my acumen and intuition? What about that?"

He didn't answer of course, gripped as he was by the dogs and the folding. I raised my hand to ask about the missing blue paper even though the room was dark, but when no one saw me I decided to stand up and walk to the front of the room to ask and maybe sign in while I was up there.

"I didn't receive a piece of blue paper," I said. "I was out in the hallway taking a phone call and I was skipped over. I was talking to my girlfriend about my pay being docked because I was late to this training, but I wasn't actually late, you see. I had only forgotten to sign in. I've been here the whole time, and I've taken this same training before anyway, so even if I was late, which I wasn't, I would already be caught up. Anyhow, I just need some blue paper." I discovered myself to be sweating, almost out of breath from my attempts at an explanation of myself.

"I'm not sure we have any blue paper left for you."

"You're out of the blue paper?"

She glanced at the empty table next to her and said, "It seems that way."

"Does someone have an extra page? Did two pages stick together maybe? Can we check?"

"Sorry, no. Besides, it doesn't matter for you anymore anyway because the video will be over soon. It's too late to start folding anything now."

"Too late?"

"Yes."

"This is just a misunderstanding," I stammered. "We're misunderstanding each other. I need to pass the training this time. This is my livelihood on the line here, my relationship with my girlfriend."

"We all have things at stake, sir, so if you don't mind

taking your seat again we're going to move on to the next phase of training momentarily."

"Can I at least sign in to prove that I was here?"

She pointed to the sign-in sheet on the table next to her and I hunched over it to look for my name, but it wasn't on there.

"My name isn't on here," I said.

"Then just sign at the bottom and print your name next to it."

I felt my pockets for a pen and realized I'd left mine back at my seat.

"Can I borrow your pen?" I asked.

After the IPF we were given a fifteen-minute break, so I offered to buy my colleague a bag of chips from the vending machine for letting me copy his notes.

"So my girlfriend called me," I said, slipping a dollar into the machine. "She said I got a letter in the mail from Kennard that my pay had been docked." The vending machine expelled my dollar bill back out again like it didn't taste good, like a baby rejecting food.

"Docked?"

"Yeah, for being late to the training today." I spread the dollar bill out against the glass of the vending machine to try and smooth it out, straining to massage it flat. "Can you believe that?" I tried to insert the dollar bill again, but we watched the machine consider it briefly, then slide it back out again as another person came up behind us in line. "What is going on here?" I said, referring to the dollar bill, growing embarrassed. I decided to exchange that dollar bill for the only other one in my wallet, thinking I could at least buy my colleague something. I tried to insert that one into the machine next, but this time the machine wouldn't even take it in, wouldn't even give it a look.

I turned to the man standing behind us and apologized before I tried the bill again one more time.

"I don't mind buying my own chips," said my colleague impatiently when he saw that the machine wasn't going to take it. My colleague pulled out his own dollar from his wallet then reached around me and put it easily into the machine, forcing me to step aside. He pressed the combination for barbeque potato chips and we all watched them unspiral from their shelf before falling, and then my colleague bent over and removed them from the bottom of the vending machine. After him, the man behind us stepped up next and inserted his own dollar bill into the machine with ease and then pressed the combination for nacho chips.

I looked at my colleague and said, "Can I trade you one of my dollars for one of your dollars?"

"That was my only dollar bill," he said, tossing a chip into his mouth.

"How about you?" I said, addressing the man reaching for the nacho chips. "Can we trade dollar bills?"

"Sorry," he said. "I'm out of cash."

The two of them stood there eating from their bags of chips chatting with each other as I tried to flatten out my dollar bill one more time. It obviously wasn't the machine, which I had just witnessed accepting money, it was something about me it was rejecting. It felt strangely personal, like even the vending machines were on Kennard's side. Next to me, I heard them eating chips and discussing the folding of their blue paper and then my colleague told him about how I didn't even bother to fold one at all, the two of them sharing a laugh about it all while I tried inserting my dollar again. I watched it go all the way in, my hope rising briefly, before it came sliding back out again, rejected.

"We better head back in," said my colleague, glancing at his wristwatch, crunching on his chips. "Time is almost up."

Back in the training room again we were all informed that the air-conditioning had apparently broken sometime in the last twenty minutes. For me it had become noticeably warmer already once we were all in there again, expelling our carbon dioxide into the air, sweating in our business attire.

"You believe this?" I said to my colleague. I was patting my forehead with the cuff of my sportcoat.

"Believe what?"

"This whole air-conditioner thing?"

"You think they're lying to us?"

"It's typical of them. I remember this part from before. I think this is the part where they try to sweat us out."

"I feel pretty comfortable, actually," said my colleague, sniffing proudly. I could smell his barbeque breath, enhanced somehow by the rising heat of the room.

I looked around and everyone else was carrying on as if the air conditioner was working just fine and they weren't lying straight to our faces. I realized that everyone else, including my colleague next to me, was absolutely okay with the ongoing farce happening at the front of the room, so I was forced to conclude that it must have been me with the problem. I don't know what got into me, but everything suddenly seemed like cardboard. Everything felt so stupid.

As the slideshow presentation rolled on up front, I found myself looking out the window next to me. I couldn't help it. I no longer cared what they were saying up front, and I was gripped by these two small birds kind of hop-flying through the branches of a large tree outside, going a little up, a little down, and then around, obviously flirting with each other, and I just really found myself wanting to be one of the two birds. I imagined the other bird to be my girlfriend, and if it were up to me we would live in those kinds of moments forever, chasing each other around the kitchen table in our underwear.

"I want to be a bird," I blurted towards my colleague. "I want to be able to do that."

He glanced at me sidewise while at the front of the room one of the presenters was discussing some line graph, pointing at certain segments of it where it either sloped up or down more dramatically than other segments and explaining why it went up or down and which direction was the desired direction for the company. Who cares anyway? I didn't. Not then and not ever, if I was being honest. It was the same set of slides with the same line graphs on them that I had seen the last time I did the training, so instead of watching the presentation again, I looked out the window, watching the birds circling the tree, jealous of their freedom and their obvious love for one another.

As I watched them I began to imagine the feeling of warm sunshine on my face. I closed my eyes and imagined myself outside for once, lying peacefully on the bow of a gleaming white yacht. I imagined a tickling breeze blowing over my tanned skin, imagined the sweet smell of suntan oil in the air, listened to the motherly sloshing of the water, and felt the sweet solitude of being adrift in the middle of the ocean, floating freely. Anyway, somewhere in there I guess I put my head down and fell asleep, but after what could have only been a few minutes at the most, my phone buzzed me out of it with a jolt.

I slipped it out and saw it was another text from my boss. He had sent a picture of me sleeping face down on the table, my head resting like an egg on my folded arms, taken from outside the very same window I had been watching the birds through, and from that moment on I knew I was screwed.

I knew I wouldn't be passing the training and that suddenly my whole life was at risk of disintegrating.

I looked out the window thinking that maybe he would still be standing there taking photos, perhaps waiting for me to wake up so he could stare me down, strip me of my pay some more, fire me on the spot and call me a Fuckstick again in front of everyone, really embarrass me, but when I looked over he wasn't there.

I turned to my colleague and said, "Hey, did you happen to notice Kennard standing outside the window taking pictures of me just now?"

"No. I've been paying attention to what's going on up front, not looking out windows."

"Look at this." I showed him the picture on my phone and he glanced at it, sidewise again. "Can he do that?"

"It's proof."

"Proof of what?"

"That maybe you are a Fuckstick like he said, sleeping right through it all, not taking any notes."

"You know what?" I snapped, feeling betrayed. "I thought you were my colleague. I thought you were on my side."

My phone buzzed in my pocket again—this time it was a text message from Kenndra. I swiped the screen to read it.

"Are you sleeping through training???" it said. Behind the three question marks I remember it had a little yellow face with steam coming out of its ears, and my heart sank. Kennard had gotten the picture to her too somehow, no doubt chipping away at me anyway he could.

I texted back, "How did Kennard get your phone number?"

She texted back a few seconds later, "He came to the

door and showed me himself."

I realized with a shudder I must have been napping longer than I thought.

I turned to my colleague and whispered, "My girlfriend just texted me that Kennard went over to my house."

My phone buzzed again, another text from Kenndra. It said, "Kennard was right, you ARE a Fuckstick," followed by a frowning yellow face with tiny tears streaming from its downturned eyes, then next thing I knew, they announced that lunch had been delivered.

Boxed lunches from a local deli: We had our choice of turkey, ham, or tuna sandwiches, each with a bag of chips, a cookie, and a pickle to go with it. I asked for a turkey sandwich, but they had just run out of those, of course, so I said, "Well how about ham?" and they asked me what I thought about tuna instead. I told them I didn't think much of it, but I took a box back to my table anyway and sat down next to my colleague, who was spreading mayonnaise on a turkey sandwich. "How did you get a turkey sandwich?" I asked.

"What do you mean?"

"They were out when I asked. Now I'm stuck with tuna."

"What's wrong with tuna?"

"It's my least favorite. I wanted turkey."

"Are you asking me to switch sandwiches with you?"

"No."

"Are you sure? I'll switch with you if it means that much."

"Thanks but no thanks. I don't want your sandwich. I'll suffer through the tuna," I said. The time to socialize was only as long as it took for people in attendance to receive a boxed lunch and return to their seats, and then our attention was called back to Required Training again. Before they started up officially though, one of the presenters took a moment to announce an update on the air conditioning only to say that due to city traffic the repairman would not be able to arrive for some time, and so nothing had changed, and furthermore, nothing much was expected to change anytime soon, which felt like a metaphor for my life at that point.

I didn't know it then of course, but my life was about to change a great deal.

The rest of the day after lunch I remember it felt like fate consuming me, the feeling of being overcome by something I couldn't resist or reverse. Up front, they started up with the next part of their presentation, which required us to answer a hypothetical question that I can't remember anymore but had something to do with bears. I had started to write something down when I remember my phone buzzing again, another text from Kenndra. I swiped the screen and it revealed a selfie of her and Kennard lying in bed together, the sheets a mess around them, pillows scattered, her head resting in the nook of my boss's shoulder while my boss gave me the middle finger. Below the picture it said, "Don't bother coming home anymore. We're through."

I texted back, "WTF?" in capital letters and stared at my phone waiting for a reply. I could barely think. I turned to my colleague and said, "Look at this!" in a furious whisper, and showed him the photo of Kenndra lying in bed with Kennard. "Is he allowed to do this?"

Before he could say anything, she texted me back. "I'm with Kennard now," she wrote, "He wins again," all followed by a smiling-face emoji, an emoji face in sunglasses, and a thumbs up.

I turned to my colleague exasperated and said furiously, "My girlfriend is cheating on me with Kennard!"

"Do you mind?" he snapped back at me. "I'm trying to finish my response here."

"Did you even hear what I said?"

"I did, yes, but why do you keep expecting me to care about it? Is she my girlfriend? Is it my life that's falling apart? That kind of thing is going on all the time in all parts of the world—Now if you don't mind."

"This could happen to you too, you know."

"No it can't because I'm not like you. I'm not a Fuckstick like you are."

My colleague turned his back to me and one of the presenters gave the room a one-minute warning to finish their responses. My colleague huffed in annoyance, his frustration clearly directed at me, and then he hurriedly scribbled something down on his paper. On mine, I wrote a few sentences about how I no longer gave a shit about any of this anymore, and then I signed it. I felt my phone buzz in my pocket again, so I took it out and swiped the screen. It was a message from my now ex-girlfriend.

"Kennard wanted me to tell you that you're fired, too," she said, followed by an emoji picture of an ax and an angry red face, the same that my boss sent me that morning, and the last thing I remember was staring at that text message for a few seconds, my head spinning, my eyes crossing, the smell of something burning coming into my nose, wondering what was happening to me, and then I guess I just started smashing my face into the table in front of almost thirty people. That's the part I stop remembering from.

After the reconstructive surgeries and the lengthy recovery, shortly after I finally came-to in the hospital bed, I was staring out the window one sunny afternoon when Kennard and Kenndra came walking in, dressed like they were going to church, my ex-girlfriend holding a bouquet of yellow roses in front of her as if she thought we could still be friends.

"These are for you," she said, laying the roses on my chest like I was lying in a coffin.

Kennard was standing next to her with his arm around her waist like I used to do, staring at me with a disturbed look on his face. As if she was putting words to his expression, Kenndra said, "You really did a number on yourself, Dan."

"You're much thinner," said Kennard. "Are they feeding you anything in here?"

All I could do was stare at them and blink my eyes, but I wanted to tell them both that even though it didn't look like it, I was actually better than ever. I wanted to tell them that they could have each other, that I was the real winner here, that I had advanced in my life more profoundly than they ever would and grown tremendously as a person since last they saw me, contrary to my appearance. I wasn't a Fuckstick anymore, that's for sure. I had done something incredible that day, something that neither of them would ever have the courage to do, which was escape it all for good. I wanted to tell them that I was a bird now and that this was my happy ending, and I was going to live my life out in the trees away from everything, but of course it was impossible to speak.

I grabbed a notebook from my bedside table and wrote, "Thank You!" on it in big letters and then raised it up for the two of them to see. They were horrified. From my bed, I made the best grin I could, which was hardly even noticeable, and then I put the notepad down and started throwing the flowers at them one at a time, aiming for their faces and backing them out of the room until they were gone forever and I was finally free.

Kennardo Goes Green

I remember it was really early morning and I was out cold because I had gone to bed so goddamn late again the night before, but here's the thing—the bedroom of my second-floor apartment is right above the outside dumpsters of our apartment complex.

Anyway, it's barely daylight out when all of a sudden my eyes explode open at the sound of some asshole emptying what must have been hundreds of glass bottles and aluminum cans into the metal dumpster right below my bedroom window. Now I can handle a little noise sometimes, I even got a slight monthly discount for taking that specific apartment, but this was beyond a normal person to do. It was so obnoxious that I actually got out of bed to look out the window and see who it was, and what do I see? Some freak in a baggy brown jacket with long red shoes on and a bright white face and red nose standing amongst a scattering of empty green recycling bins.

As soon as I appeared at the window, that clown looked

straight up at me, like he was expecting me to appear at just that moment—like it was all scripted—and I felt like I had unwittingly become a performer in some show he was putting on for himself. That's when I knew it was intentional, that it was all done on purpose. Who has that many bins of bottles and cans anyway? If I didn't have to put on clothes and go down a flight of stairs and around the backside of the building to get to him, I would have punched his lights out and ripped his stupid little puffball nose to pieces right in front him.

He stared up at me for a few more seconds, grinning, revealing a small gap between his two front teeth, and then he waved at me, some over-exaggerated clown wave, trying to be friendly all of a sudden, and I thought, "Seriously? You're gonna wave at me right now?" I shook my fist at him and flipped him off, and then I went back to sleep again. That was the last I ever saw of him.

Because of Dan Kennard

The gray-brown clouds were peeking in from beyond the horizon where I have been hiding them since the beginning, waiting this whole time for the proper moment to put them to use. But now, because of Dan Kennard and his unhealthy habit of eating candy bars for breakfast each morning, I found that the opportunity was fast approaching.

You see, down on the page, it turns out that Dan Kennard has just emerged from a convenience store a few blocks from his office and is now walking down a sidewalk in Sunset City near 108th Street and Equator Avenue. Lately, he has begun stopping into this convenience store on his way to work every morning to buy a candy bar, a candy bar that combines a chocolate outer layer with an inside of crunchy, flaky peanut butter, the mouth-watering thought of which had become too much for him to resist anymore. He used to be better. He used to eat apples and bananas for breakfast, or yogurt with berries, or eggs with sautéed peppers and onions, he used to *care* about the quality of his breakfast. If you were able to ask Dan directly, he would tell you that even though he knows it's not a very good thing to eat for breakfast—and he daily considers buying something better like maybe a granola bar or a bag of trail mix—he could no longer help himself. But like a lot of us, he is suffering in the tension between when it is appropriate to eat well and when it's okay not to. The problem is that in the world of this story, not eating well is made so, so easy that it's hard for anyone to resist. It was almost like his actions and behaviors were out of his control completely because they were, and yet even so, if he were confronted about it, he would freely take the blame for them and repent profusely for what he ended up causing to happen on that last day. The truth is, though, it was all a set up, an opportunity for me to finally bring in the clouds.

Like every morning in recent memory, upon emerging from the convenience store, Dan began tearing away the wrapper on the candy bar as he snaked his way through the sidewalk traffic towards his job at Klyber Corp. He was running a few minutes late again, as usual, moving through the people until he finally arrived at the intersection where he would cross to his office building. Like every morning before this one, he stood impatiently waiting for the signal to change, and as he took the last few bites of his candy bar, he squirmed his way over to the nearby trashcan on the corner and tossed the wrapper towards the opening. However, a very unlikely thing happened that morning that had never happened before: He missed.

He didn't mean to miss it, let's get that part out of the way, and believe me when I tell you that I made sure he felt some small amount of shame as he watched the wrapper flutter over the opening and just keep going, but because he was a character in my story his actions weren't his own, so there was nothing for him to do about it. I certainly wasn't going to send him chasing after it and risk getting him run over by the passing traffic, so all he could really do was what any of us would have done, which was watch helplessly as it fluttered through the air, across the street, and away from him.

For a few moments, still waiting for the signal to cross the intersection, he watched as the wrapper was carried up the sidewalk by the unusually strong breezes I was sending through there that morning, which had further combined with the rush of passing cars to send the wrapper whirling down the opposite sidewalk until it eventually drifted out of sight. It ended up ricocheting off a utilities pole half a block away before finally settling permanently into a shadowed corner where a concrete wall met perpendicular with a chain-link fence, but it was already too late, the process of ending had already begun.

I had already decided to replace the normal breezes that had once accompanied most mornings with strong gusty winds, but the wind isn't the only thing I was interfering with. I was interfering with other things too, leaving clues to my existence everywhere, making my presence felt more than ever as I pushed all my characters through their final pages together.

As the last day of Sunset City unspooled from my brain into these sentences, the sounds of sirens could now be heard echoing in from the distance. Normally Dan would have had his earbuds in and probably not heard them, but because he was the main character I made it so that he had forgotten them at home that day, leaving them on his kitchen counter as he rushed out the front door, and so only a few minutes after missing the trashcan he heard them start ringing loud and clear, the sound traveling crisply between the concrete buildings, moving and circling around the city as the firetrucks and ambulances raced towards their destinations.

After he had arrived at his floor, he entered his office and sat down in front of his cubicle and said, "Morning everybody. Lots of sirens out there today. Did anyone notice the sirens?" He looked around at a few of his colleagues nearby, but no one had acknowledged him or the sirens and he got the strange impression that they were all angry with him, but what for? He wiped the corners of his mouth with a napkin to make sure the chocolate was gone and tossed it straight into the trashcan under his cubicle desk.

It had only been fifteen or so minutes since his candy wrapper had permanently settled into the corner of the concrete wall and the chain-link fence about three blocks away from his present location on the thirty-third floor of the Executive Tower, but it was enough time for Dan to log online and find out about what I was doing to all the airplanes and the birds, which would also end up explaining the sirens.

Upon reading the news, Dan spun in his desk chair towards his colleague Gary in the cubicle next to him and found him typing, his white earbuds tucked neatly into his ears. Dan reached over and tapped him on the shoulder to get his attention and Gary turned towards him startled, and clearly annoyed at being interrupted. He removed an earbud. "What is it? What do you want?"

"Did you hear about the planes?" asked Dan.

"Yeah, I heard about the planes. We all did. It's horrible and we've already talked about it. Everyone who was here on time was talking about the planes falling just a few minutes ago, right before you came in."

"I don't remember anything like this happening before."

"Birds too, right, Denise? Denise mentioned that

earlier, before you came in."

Denise leaned back in her chair, emerging into view from her cubicle two cubicles down from Dan and said, "I read online just now that some guy in Midland got the beak straight into the top of the head while he was walking to his car. His wife found his dead body halfway between their front door and the driveway in a puddle of blood and feathers. She's posting pictures of it. Can you believe that?"

"Could have been anybody," said Gary reflectively.

"Yeah, you would think they would sort of flutter to the ground, or spin, but no—beak first the whole way," added Denise.

"Did anyone try to explain why?" asked Dan.

"Why what?" said Denise.

"Why this is happening."

Even though for me it felt like I was waving at them from some other level of the universe, naturally they did not pick up on the fact that it was me, the other Dan Kennard, flicking them out of the sky with my giant god-like fingers, making my presence known to everyone clear as day.

A little later on, I cracked thunder so booming that it rattled the entire Executive Tower, causing the lights to flicker briefly and sending vibrations up through their feet, while outside my clouds were gathering ominously.

Dan stood up from his desk and went over to the window that looked out upon the expanse of Sunset City below, an action that also happened to be a direct violation of Klyber's office conduct policy, part of which read: "Thou shall not leave thou desk chair without the permission of a Superior." Klyber Corp, like a lot of other corporations at the time, had a stringent set of rules to be followed that were designed and implemented to produce a maximum effort and efficiency from the people subjected to them, eliminate any form of interference from an employee through a series of escalating consequences, while simultaneously steering clear of legal troubles, but in that moment Dan didn't care about any of that stuff.

Looking out the window, he saw how I had made the skies grow overcast, my unnatural-looking gray-brown clouds slowly materializing over the dome of the city and changing the course of the morning forever. I cracked more thunder down from the sky and let what everyone thought was rain begin to shower down on everything, using the gusts of wind to pound the windows with it, and all of a sudden Sunset City found itself with quite the storm on its hands.

Dan looked back towards his cubicle to find his boss, Lemming, standing behind his empty desk chair, clipboard in hand, no doubt writing him up for Inefficiency Infractions, shaking his head in disappointment as he scribbled, but Dan turned back to the window anyway and observed the city outside as the rain continued beating against the glass.

Scanning the horizon for plumes of smoke, he looked for the fallen planes, but the combination of rain streaking the window and the gray haze that had settled over everything outside caused the normally sharp-lined geometry of the city to look more like a watercolor painting, every edge of every thing appearing to blur and smear and overlap, so that it became difficult to discern much of anything.

Back at his cubicle later on, Dan suddenly became concerned with the idea that he hadn't yet heard from his girlfriend Kenndra that morning, knowing that she usually texts him a little something-or-other before lunchtime at the latest, a quick hey-how-you-doing text message that he would then return during his lunch hour when they were allowed to use their phones.

Because of an overwhelming feeling that something was wrong, that his relation to the world had suddenly become tilted or distorted somehow, Dan sat awhile searching his mind for reasons why she might not have texted him yet: Maybe he had said something that morning before leaving for work that had upset her somehow, but he couldn't think of what it might have been. Maybe, he thought to himself, it was because he woke up too late to make it to the required training Klyber held the previous weekend. He remembered that when he finally did wake up and walked into the kitchen in his underwear, he poured himself a cup of coffee and said, "I'm not gonna make it now. Why bother?" He remembered how she glared at him when he said that.

The truth, however, was that it wasn't any of those things. The truth was that Kenndra simply didn't think to text him that morning; in fact, she didn't think of him at all.

It turns out that I had positioned Kenndra somewhere on the opposite side of the city, almost as far away from Dan at the moment as she could be. She was sitting in her car, listening to music and waiting at a red light, waiting for the signal to change for going on seven or eight minutes at that point when she heard her phone buzz inside her purse. She reached over to the passenger seat and took it out, saw that it was a message from Dan asking if she had heard about the planes. She swiped it open.

"No," she texted back. "I'm stuck at a red light that won't change. Nothing is moving," followed by a distressed-looking emoji face. "Should you be texting right now?" she typed, holding the phone in her hands and waiting for his reply buzz.

"Planes are falling from the sky everywhere!" he texted back, followed by a wide-eyed emoji face. "Birds too! I wanted to make sure you were safe. Where are you?" he added, followed by the tiny emoji picture of a radiating pink heart. He didn't normally use such cutesy emojis in his text messages, but because he had their weekend argument over required training in his mind again and he was feeling vaguely guilty about something he couldn't quite identify, he wanted to at least make sure she knew he loved her. This extra effort to show his love for Kenndra came at the perfect time, too, because she had been spending some of that seven or eight minutes at the red light debating whether or not Dan was the kind of man she could see herself spending the rest of her life with.

"I'm on the opposite side of town. It's pouring rain and thundering," she typed, followed by a line of emoji lightning bolts, even though I hadn't included any lightning yet in my descriptions.

Back at his desk Dan typed discreetly: "Here 2."

She read his message and then each of them just sat where they were, Dan slumped at his desk, Kenndra leaning against the window of her car on the other side of the city still waiting for the light to change, both of them falling lifeless for a few moments like abandoned puppets. They both held their phones in their palms, neither one sure how to proceed or what to say next, each of them sitting in their respective locations, pondering each other, pondering the infinite red light and the rain coming down more powerfully by the minute, until Kenndra snapped up suddenly at the sound of three fire trucks racing through the intersection in front of her, red lights spinning and sirens blaring, rushing towards some catastrophe in the distance.

For the rest of the day after that, I made it so that Dan would have a hard time concentrating on his work. No one in the story knew it yet, but my clouds would continue to pour their liquid down steadily right up until the end, and I would keep roiling the thunder from up here beyond the clouds, and all I would let Dan do was stare anxiously towards the window from his desk chair, watching the water run down the glass in glimmery rivulets, and then—how long had his boss been standing there?

"Come with me, Dan. We need to talk."

"May I stand from my seat, sir?"

"Don't pretend to care about protocol all of a sudden. Stand up and come with me."

His boss turned and began walking back towards his office expecting Dan to follow him, which he did because he had to, because he couldn't afford to lose his job, and because of Kenndra too. He followed his boss down a hallway thinking about how he could explain away his actions, but he was too rushed to come up with anything before they arrived at his door.

As they entered his private office, Lemming said, "Close the door. Take a seat." He was speaking sternly, avoiding eye contact, holding the expression of someone who was thinking about the words he wanted to use to say whatever it was he was about to say, trying to find the right angle on things to begin a difficult conversation. "Do you know why I brought you in here?" he asked, settling into his squeaky leather chair.

"Sir, I imagine it could be because of my transgressions earlier at the window, for which I apologize. I had just read about the planes falling, and I got a bad feeling in my gut. I had to look for the plumes to see for myself."

"The bad feeling in your gut is from that candy bar you eat every morning for breakfast," he snapped. "Don't think we don't know about that because we do. We know all about you and your candy bar breakfast, but the window business isn't the only thing we need to discuss. You missed required training this past weekend too, you're staring out the window or texting under your desk all the time instead of working, and to top it all off, you were late again today. Did you think we wouldn't notice these things?"

"What required training? I didn't know about that."

"Of course you did. We sent an email about it every day for a week. Are you lying straight to my face now? Should we add that to the list?"

"No, sir."

"Well then are you checking your email?"

"Sure I am. All the time. Now that I think about it, I guess I just thought I did all the required trainings already. I have attended a lot of required trainings during my time at Klyber. I have a whole binder of certificates I can show you."

"There are always going to be new trainings, Kennard, right up until the day you die, so don't play stupid with me. You blew it off, plain and simple, you made a conscious and deliberate decision not to go."

"It was an honest mistake."

"Sure it was. And I'm a goose. I have feathers and a beak, right? My brain is tiny like a bird?"

"Sir?"

"Do you know what time work starts?"

"Eight o'clock."

"Eight o'clock, that's right. So why are you clocking in after that every day?"

"I don't know, sir."

"Is that an honest mistake too? That you somehow, after all these years of working and your binder full of certificates, that you still, against all odds, don't even know when work starts?"

"I'm snoozing one too many times I guess. One night my phone didn't get plugged in properly and the battery died. Phones are everything these days. I think I need a new cord, but they're so expensive. I'll stop snoozing though. I'll check to make sure my phone is plugged in. I'll splurge on a new cord. I promise."

"Here's the deal, Kennard: If you clock in even one nano-second after eight for the rest of this month, you're fired. If you're running late, don't even bother coming the rest of the way in, just turn around and go home. Don't try to call either because I'm going to give zero shits about whatever excuse you will have come up with. Do you understand?"

"I'll stop snoozing. I'll be on time from now on."

"I'll believe it when I see it," said Lemming dismissively. "By the way, don't plan on going anywhere for lunch because I've ordered everyone a sandwich."

"A Working Lunch?"

"That's right. The way I figure it you have some time to make up to the folks at Klyber because we are the people who make your paycheck possible every other week. We're your livelihood. We are your rent payment and your grocery bill. Klyber is everything to you whether you realize it or not, so until you can show a minimal level of respect towards your job and your colleagues that make your entire existence possible as a comfortable, almost middle-class person, we're going to have Working Lunches for everyone."

"Please don't punish everyone else because of me, sir. I can change."

"It's too late to change now. Besides, I already sent an email out to everyone in the office this morning. I wrote, 'If Kennard clocks in after eight o'clock today, it's Working

Lunches for everyone the rest of the week.' Everyone knows it was your fault. It's out there now. Working Lunches all week because of Dan Kennard."

Klyber hadn't had a Working Lunch in a long time, and so everyone at the office had become used to going out in order to escape the confines of their cubicles and chat with one another more freely before returning for the final stretch of the afternoon, so the Working Lunch punishment because of Dan Kennard was a real miserable blow to the office morale.

If you were to ask the other employees, despite the incredible downpour outside, going out of the office for lunch was probably the thing they most looked forward to each day other than going home at the end, but now, because of Dan Kennard, they would be eating over their keyboards for the rest of the week.

Tragically though, all of their resentment towards Dan would be wasted because, unlike us, they didn't know that there wouldn't be any rest of the week. For a lot of the people in the office that day the boxed lunch from the deli, which was only just okay, would end up being their last meal because by that evening, when things really started to fall apart, most people had completely lost their appetite for food.

When Lunch Hour officially began, Lemming wheeled the boxed lunches into the cubicle area on a metal cart and then stood with his arms crossed sternly over his chest like he was sizing everyone up, like an uptight ship captain, while an employee from the deli wheeled the cart through the office handing out the boxes. Lemming called for everyone's attention.

"As you all already know, because of Dan Kennard over there, who just can't seem to take this job seriously enough to show up to trainings and clock in on time, and who regularly defies office protocol regarding personal use of technology, we will be instituting Working Lunch Rules for the rest of the week.

"Since it has been a long time since our last Working Lunch, allow me to review the rules. First of all, it is what it is called, that is, a Working Lunch, which for any new people means that you are expected to be eating the meal I've bought for you and continuing your work at the same time. The standard office conduct rules remain in effect regarding use of personal technology, with the exception of headphones, which studies have shown increase concentration and focus, and which Klyber encourages. However," and he looked at Dan as he added this last part, "there will be no texting, no talking, and no leaving your seats during this Working Lunch except to use the restroom, for which you must ask permission via the Insta-Chat system, as usual. Does anyone have questions?"

No one spoke and the only sounds at the moment were the rain tinkling against the office window and the howling of the wind outside. The cart, meanwhile, had gone around to everyone else first and arrived at Dan's cubicle last, which was just as his boss had secretly instructed, and so by then he didn't have a choice of sandwich anymore because there was only one box left. It was placed in front of him, and he nearly gagged when he saw that the label said "Tuna Fish".

At the front of the office, Lemming concluded by saying, "If there are no questions, then the Working Lunch is officially underway," and then he checked his watch to mark the time. As soon as Dan opened his box, I made his phone buzz from the back corner of his desk, but of course he couldn't check it now; Lemming was circling the office like a shark and Dan was smart enough to know that having your hands anywhere but on your computer mouse or around your sandwich was blood in the water for him.

Naturally, Dan figured it was Kenndra checking in on him, seeing how his day was going, expecting him to text her back like he always did between the hours of twelve and one when they were allowed to use their phones freely, but she didn't know he had caused a Working Lunch for everyone. If she did, she would obviously be disappointed in him, especially since missing the required training was a factor in it, and she would likely begin questioning herself and their relationship even more than she already was. Did she really want to stay with a man who makes things so much worse for the people around him? Dan imagined that now she would be wondering why he wasn't responding to her like he usually did at that time of day, which he could easily see leading to something later on when he would be forced to tell her the truth of the situation. He could feel his heart racing.

He really wanted to read the message and respond to her so that all of that could be avoided, but there was no way he could let himself get caught reading a text message during a Working Lunch that he was responsible for, especially not after the meeting he had with Lemming earlier and with so much now on the line. But truth be told, he couldn't take his mind off of it.

Like so many of us out in the real world, it was giving him anxiety not to check, not to respond, not to know. Touching his phone was all he could think about. Did she ever get where she was trying to go that morning? He wanted to know. He wanted to know everything, and on top of it all he felt compelled to apologize to her for something too, to say sorry about being who he was and apologize for his actions going all the way back to the beginning of their relationship, even though he didn't have anything specific in mind other than the required training. Now that he couldn't talk and text with her, he wanted to tell her more than ever about how he felt: like something was wrong with him. He tried to look away from the phone and the blinking green light that was calling out to him to swipe at the screen and focus on something else to distract his mind from the rising anxiety and nausea coming over him, overwhelmed as he was with implacable guilt, feeling the resentment from the rest of the office palpable in the air. He tried to focus on his lunch.

He examined the box his lunch came in and noticed that it was soggy around the edges, probably from being transported through the downpour, and it was likely to begin tearing apart at the seams pretty soon just like he was and just like my world was doing outside. He picked up the bottle of unlabeled water that came with his sandwich, but it was dripping wet with condensation, and so water went running down his wrist and forearm the same way it was doing on the window. He twisted the cap off and swigged from the bottle, put it down again, and then wiped off his forearm and wrist with a napkin. He picked up the tuna sandwich with the idea of forcing himself to eat it, but it was apparent right away once he held it to his mouth he couldn't do it.

He dropped it back into the box and looked at the chips that he didn't like either, and he realized he wasn't going to be able to make himself eat anything. The idea of combining the taste of tuna and salt and vinegar chips in his mouth, possibly for the rest of the day, suddenly made him a little light-headed. He began to feel like he would fall out of his desk chair if he didn't close he eyes and try to center himself, and then he found his mind drifting back to his phone again. The urge for him to check it returned, more powerful and intoxicating than ever, and it was suddenly the only thing that seemed like it could make him feel better. He just wanted to pick it up, swipe the screen, read the message, and then put it back again out of sight, a quick hit to make the world tolerable again.

He looked around the office to try and discreetly locate the positioning of his boss so he could calculate whether or not he had time to swipe his screen and read what he assumed was Kenndra's text, talking himself into it despite the obvious risk involved. If he were to get caught on his phone after everything else that day, it would be perfectly suitable for Lemming to fire him on the spot and have him escorted out by building security.

Nonetheless, he checked first to his left while simultaneously letting the hand he was supposed to be using to hold his sandwich slide ever so slowly towards his phone at the back corner of his desk. When he didn't see his boss anywhere to the left, he turned back to his right again, his hand cupping the phone, his brain feeling a rush of excitement at the touch of its smooth edges, and then he immediately felt the presence of another human body next to him. It was Lemming, standing behind him with his arms crossed.

"Everything okay over here, Kennard?"

He snatched his hand away from the phone like he had burned himself on it and said, with his voice quivering, "Yes sir, everything is okay over here."

Lemming leaned over him and looked down at his desk. "Is there something wrong with your sandwich?"

"Honestly, sir, tuna is my least favorite kind of sandwich, and the bun is damp from the rain."

Everyone in the office turned to look at them now, sensing a possible confrontation, which, honestly, was the last thing Dan wanted. He couldn't afford to lose his job because ultimately what Lemming said was right: it was his whole life, and the loss of his job most certainly meant the loss of Kenndra too, along with everything else in his life. On top of that, because there were so many people in the world, jobs were hard to find anymore, especially jobs that paid a reasonable salary, and so at the end of the day, so to speak, Klyber had him trapped unless he was willing to give up everything else in his life. It goes without saying that they could find someone to replace him at his cubicle by the next day if they had to, not knowing, of course, that there wouldn't be a next day. But Dan wasn't going to quit, and he wasn't trying to get fired either.

"Is this some kind of protest, Kennard?"

"Protest? No, sir."

"What about the bag of salt and vinegar chips? Are you going to eat those?"

"No, sir. Those are also my least favorite flavor of chip. They make me nauseous somehow."

"Salt and vinegar chips make you nauseous?" Lemming looked at him skeptically, like he was a piece of shit.

"Ever since I was a kid, sir. Something about the smell of the vinegar, I think. I'm actually feeling a bit light-headed at the moment thinking about it."

"You're feeling light-headed because you need to eat real food, Kennard. You can't just eat candy bars and breath the air all day. The air is zero calories per serving, and in here it's probably not even that good for you."

"What does that mean?"

"It doesn't matter. Listen to me: At Klyber, we're only as strong as the weakest link, and right now that's you. There's a thousand people out there right now," he said, pointing towards the window and the watercolor expanse of city. "There's a thousand people out there right now who would love to have your job, and who would love to eat a free tuna sandwich and chips while they worked. Do you get that?"

"I understand, sir."

"Do you though?"

"Sure I do. I get it," he stammered.

"Look at you—you're delirious, Kennard. You have dark circles under your eyes, too. You look pale. You need to eat something," and then he turned to everyone else and said, "You might want to say your goodbyes to Kennard now, everyone. He's coming apart at the seams."

"Permission to stand, sir."

"What for?"

"I need to use the restroom immediately. I think I'm going to throw up."

"Throw up what? You haven't eaten anything."

"Sir, please."

Lemming considered it for a moment, looked Dan over again. "Fine, go," he said. "And when you're done puking up water and candy bars, try getting some actual work done, or this is going to be your last day here."

On the other side of town the red light never became green again, in fact I had made every stoplight in the city permanently red, and because of the traffic piling up in every direction, it seemed as if everything were suddenly coming to a stop at once. After a while, people finally lost their patience and began to abandon their cars in the street, hopping out into the downpour and dashing off somewhere to take cover. For Kenndra, though, it was a falling bird smashing beak-first into her windshield that finally forced her out.

Frozen in shock, she watched the bird slide down the wet windshield towards the hood of her car, its wings bent outward in an awkward direction, its beady black eyes looking right at her and its feathers sticking out every which way before it got swept up in the back-and-forth of her windshield wipers. At that point, the idea of sitting in her car staring at the carcass of a dead bird spread-out and disheveled across her windshield was out of the question for her, which was really just my way of forcing the story onward. She grabbed her purse from the passenger seat, and then pushed the door open with her foot, the cold liquid hitting her immediately. As she went hurrying towards the sidewalk it was impossible not to feel the powerful strangeness of the sky above, brownish-gray and imposing, the world seeming to glow with an inner light that threatened to overtake everything if it could only be let loose.

With the liquid coming down the way it was, by the time she made it about half a block up the street, her hair and shoulders were already soaked and her feet were wet from the puddles when she came upon a coffee shop I had placed at exactly the point at which I knew she would be most likely to stop in. She ordered a cup of hot black coffee and then began the impossible task of looking for a place to sit down, the coffee shop crowded with other anonymous people escaping the rain, and she drifted towards the back of the seating area until a man named Ken saw her passing by and offered her a seat.

"Would you like to sit down with me?" he said. "Not a lot of room in here today."

She shot a glance in his direction thinking that it was Dan's voice, and when she saw him it was apparent right away that he looked eerily like him too. His beard and glasses, his side-parted haircut, the slight gap in his teeth she saw as he smiled up at her.

"Do we know each other?" she asked, intrigued.

"Not yet," he said, smiling at her. "I was idling in the car next to you down the street. I tried to get your attention as I was leaving, but you didn't notice me. Then I thought about knocking on your window, but I didn't want to scare you because then I figured you would never take me seriously. So I decided to just sit here and hope you might eventually come in, and I'll be damned if my heart didn't jump when I saw you push your way through that door."

"I'm sorry I didn't notice you."

"It's okay. You're here now. It's fate."

Under the table, I had him push a chair out with his foot as a way to invite her to sit down and so she did, barely able to help herself, and it was already a more romantic start than she had gotten off to with Dan the year before when they first met at a party and he had spilled his drink on her. Dan had drunkenly offered to trade shirts with her after that, proposing that he would wear hers and she could wear his, which, after she declined, had lead to some sloppy flirting until eventually instead of shirts they settled on exchanging phone numbers. It was a hard thing for her to admit, but even though they had done pretty well together since then, there was still the nagging question in her mind, implanted from her mother as a guideline for her adult dating life, of whether or not the person in front of her, Dan in this case, was someone she could envision spending the rest of her life with. The answer so far was not totally. On the flip side, the thought of starting all over again and being single felt too exhausting to even imagine, but sitting down across from Ken that morning, each of them with their black coffees steaming in front of them, Kenndra realized she was blushing with intrigue.

"My name is Ken," he said. "Ken Dannerd."

"I'm Kenndra," she said. "I really appreciate you offering me a seat."

"Better to sit with me than in your car, I hope," to which she agreed whole-heartedly, and then it was off to the races, so to speak. They continued to talk for another hour or so, discussing the planes and the birds and the red lights and the torrential rain and the thunder that I was continually rumbling outside, trying to figure out what it could all mean, neither of them imaginative enough to consider the idea that their world was ending because to both of them it felt more like a new beginning.

To her delight, Kenndra learned that Ken was truly funny and had a nice smile, which are two things she'd never been able to say about Dan. He also had a higher paying job and was planning on buying a house just outside the city with the money he'd been saving where he planned to live off the land as much as possible. He talked about rain barrels, solar panels, and vegetable gardens with a joy and enthusiasm that Kenndra couldn't remember Dan ever having about anything other than maybe a football game or something, all of which coalesced into Ken making Dan look pathetic in comparison.

Kenndra, meanwhile, managed to dodge the fact that she was currently in a relationship with Dan at all, and soon enough it didn't even seem to matter anymore. Ken was like a figurative bird falling into her figurative windshield from heaven above, shocking her out of one life and straight into another one. She was practically forced to trade up, Dan for Ken, and inside her brain she could hear her mind chanting, "Yes! Yes! This is the man I've been waiting for!"

They ended up talking all the way until lunchtime time when Ken suggested they walk around the corner to a restaurant he knew of, a proposal to which she quickly agreed and at which point it was safe to say that Kenndra was no longer thinking about Dan at all.

At the exact same time that was happening, Dan was hunched over the toilet in the handicap stall of the Klyber restroom, gripping the silver bar attached to the wall as a sweat broke out across his forehead, and he was feeling like his whole life coming apart, which it pretty much was.

He was staring at the rim of the toilet bowl and the dirty underside of the seat, a chill of disgust coming over him, and then he remembered with overwhelming relief that he had his phone with him. He had snatched it from his desk and put it in his pocket on his way to the bathroom and then in his brief delirium had gone and forgot all about it. He straightened up immediately and slipped it out.

He swiped at the screen, desperate to talk to Kenndra, who he realized more and more through the course of the day was the only thing in his life that he truly loved, and he was feeling terribly bad that for some reason it might already be too late to express those thoughts to her properly, but as he looked at his phone, he was stunned to find that the message he received earlier wasn't from Kenndra at all, but was actually a coupon-text from a discount shoe store.

He slipped his phone back into his pocket disappointed and splashed some water on his face, then snatched a brown paper towel from the dispenser and wiped himself dry, feeling better, feeling compelled by the events of the morning and the unrelenting reminders of the fleeting nature of life to be more aware than ever of the weight of responsibility he had toward Kenndra and their life together, which all happened to be contingent upon his having a job. As he stared at himself in the mirror, he resolved to try and be better, to live better, to eat better, to be more responsible, but of course, like anyone else attempting to repent for their own personal failings at the moment, it was all too little too late.

Surprisingly perhaps, Dan left the bathroom without ever texting Kenndra to see how she was doing, if she had ever made it where she was trying to go, if she had seen any plumes of smoke in the distance, or what had happened with the red light, mostly out of a fear that he wouldn't be able to reply to whatever it is she might say in response, and he didn't want to put himself through the mental agony of all that. He certainly didn't need to bring on any more trouble for himself by continuing to violate office protocol, and he certainly didn't want to have to explain in lengthy texts the fact that he had caused a Working Lunch for everyone, and that his job was suddenly on the line. Instead, he walked back to his cubicle where his tuna sub and potato chips were still exactly as he had left them, and despite his newfound resolve to live a better life— something that he knew required an open heart and willingness to try new things—he still found himself unable to bring himself to eat anything.

He looked around the office at his colleagues who up until that moment he always thought seemed to take their jobs too seriously, but now he found himself both admiring and envious of their work ethic, seeing now that they all understood something that he hadn't. He watched Gary next to him absorbed in his typing, his fingers moving gracefully, spiritually even, across the keyboard, completely in the Zone, switching unconsciously between the open windows on his computer screen and inputting his data with an efficiency and smoothness that Dan had yet to achieve or even tried to achieve, and then from outside I interrupted his train of thought with a cracking of thunder that caused the whole building to lose electricity for a split-second—just enough to restart everyone's computers.

"God damnit," huffed Gary, the spell of his work broken, pushing himself back from his desk. "Now I have to start all over again."

Denise leaned back into view and said, "You always have to save things, Gary. Always, always be saving."

"Thanks, Debbie. That's very helpful right now. Just the thing I need to hear. All I can think about is that I shouldn't even be here right now—I should be drinking a freakin beer at lunch. There's a parallel universe where Dan shows up to work on time for once and I'm drinking a cold beer at the bar."

"You shouldn't drink during the work day, Gary," said Denise.

"Debbie, please don't recite your fucking morals to me right now."

"I'm sorry, Gary," said Dan. "I'm really sorry."

"It's too late for all that," he retorted. "If I were you I wouldn't even bother going home tonight."

"I was thinking of buying a new pair of shoes after work. I got a coupon."

"Fuck your shoes," said Gary, staring up at the ceiling despondently as everyone's computers went through the process of restarting. "Nobody looks at those things. They should be under your desk and out of sight anyway. Have you considered the idea that you should actually spend some time at your desk once in a while instead of staring out windows and hanging out in the bathroom?"

"Take it easy, Gary," said Denise. "It's not his fault you didn't save your work."

"Debbie, please stop talking to me. This has nothing to do with me saving my work. This is all because of Dan Kennard. I don't need you defending this fuckstick. We're in this position because of him. I should be halfway into my second lunch beer right now, but because this guy can't get his life together enough to attend trainings and show up to work on time, I'm here instead of there, waiting for my computer to restart so I can do all over what I've already done. This is a kind of hell, Debbie; I just described hell. Don't go and try to make any of this my fault."

"Hey, Gary. I said I'm sorry. I'm going to be better. I'm not going to be late anymore, I promise. I'll make it up to you. Next chance we get, I'll buy you those beers myself, I promise. I owe you those beers," insisted Dan.

He had become visibly desperate to make things right with the world around him, starting with Gary and the rest of the office, who happened to feel the same way towards him at the moment, and he was ready to plead for their forgiveness, formulating apologies in his head like his life was on the line while all around him everything else continued to slip permanently out of place.

Because Dan forgot his earbuds that day rushing out of his apartment, he was forced to sit listening to the rain and the thunder and the sirens that continued to blare from the distance, each one of them feeling like a threat to his life and his relationship because even though he had decided not to text Kenndra earlier in the bathroom when he had the chance, it was hard not to recognize that she had apparently decided not to text him either, all of which is to say that I wasn't making it any easier on him.

His phone sat silently in his pocket, and I caused him to think darkly that maybe something bad had happened to her and he just hadn't found out yet, and the nervous anxiety that he thought he had rid himself of earlier in the bathroom slowly crept back into his mind again as he began to obsess over everything that could have happened, part of which included the thought that if the rain kept up (which it would), it might start to cause some pretty serious flooding, and the idea that he could somehow become trapped at work or that Kenndra could be trapped somewhere else on the other side of Sunset City seemed more and more like a real possibility. He soon found it impossible to concentrate until he knew where she was, and so he slid his phone from his pocket and decided to text Kenndra, consequences be damned.

"How's it going?" he typed quickly, before slipping the phone discreetly under his thigh and waiting with impatient expectation to feel a reply buzz come back from Kenndra. As we know though, Kenndra had forgotten about Dan completely by this point of the story, smitten as she was with Ken, and on top of that, her phone was in her purse, and her purse was on the floor underneath a restaurant table, out of sight and out of mind just like Dan was, which is a long way of saying that she wouldn't be texting him back anytime soon.

Across town, after Ken and Kenndra finished their own lunch, a lunch which Ken insisted on paying for, they emerged from the restaurant onto the sidewalk again and stood under the restaurant's tattered awning when Ken said, "Sirens. You hear that?"

They listened together through the relentless white noise of the pouring liquid that everyone still thought was rain, huddled close, so obviously enamored with each other already that their body language made it seem as if they had been dating for months, and they were certainly in no rush to separate.

"Look at these clouds," said Ken. "It's practically dark outside now."

"Do you think we should check on our cars?" asked Kenndra.

"What's the point? We might get soaked."

"It could be fun," said Kenndra. "It might make a good story one day."

"It's already a good story," replied Ken.

"Well, now what?" said Kenndra.

"My apartment happens to only be a few blocks away from here," he suggested. "I didn't get very far this morning before this whole red light thing brought us together." He paused nervously. "I have wine and soft-baked chocolate chip cookies that I just bought yesterday, and if we get stuck there for a while with the rain, I have a frozen pizza we can eat later too. I'm stocked up for the apocalypse."

"What apocalypse?" she said.

"This one. The one that's happening right now as we speak," I made him say.

"What are you talking about?"

"I'm just saying that I went grocery shopping yesterday and if the world were to somehow end up trapping us together that I'm ready for it. I have food."

She looked at him and said, "Did you know chocolate chip is my favorite kind of cookie?"

"See that?" He smiled. "It's fate. It's all fate."

Ken reached for her hand and they stepped out from under the awning of the restaurant and started back towards his apartment, but after just a few steps, it was impossible not to notice that their shoes were sticking to the sidewalk with every step, causing them to leave a trail of footprints behind them like they were walking along a beach somewhere. The people passing them in the other direction were leaving footprints too, and as they moved along together side-by-side, hand-in-hand under the stretch of sidewalk awnings, they began to notice that even the awnings were beginning to develop holes in them. By the time they arrived outside his apartment building, they were soaked, their hair wet and their shoulders wet, their socks squishy inside their also wet shoes, while I continued to shower the liquid down upon all of my creation, clapping my thunder, and eroding everything away like it was nothing more than a playground sandcastle being leveled out by the rain.

On the other side of the city, the people of Klyber could feel themselves approaching the crest of the afternoon, but looking out the window it would be easy to think it was the middle of the night.

"It's practically dark outside now," said Dan to no one in particular.

This fact created the disorienting effect for Dan that he was somehow living through a bad dream where he was at work when he should have been at home sleeping, spooning with Kenndra in their bed, but that would never happen again. Looking out the office window, Dan didn't know any more than anyone else about the impending end of the world, but even if he couldn't speak to it directly, as a rule of character he felt it coming more than anyone else did.

He turned to Gary and tapped him on the shoulder and said, "Something is wrong. We shouldn't be here right now."

Gary plucked an earbud from his ear annoyed. "What the hell are you talking about?"

"This weather, Gary. Look at the sky. Where did the sun go?"

"Are you a child? It's a storm, Dan. It will pass. It will be okay."

"What about the planes?"

"What is your obsession with these planes? Were you on one? Were you crushed underneath of one? Do you think we need all of these people anyway? The world is being overrun with people as it is. It's self-correction is what it is."

"That's pretty harsh, Gary."

"Well it's true, right?" He was suddenly fuming. "It's

the world's way of burning off excess calories or something. But as we all sit around waiting for our turn, we have work to do."

"Are you saying that people are the calories of the earth? I don't think I get that."

"Listen, I know you don't take any of this seriously, I know you don't want to work because you'd rather rush off and buy a pair of cheap shoes or whatever, but don't think that I don't take this seriously. I take this seriously as fuck, Dan, do you get that? Without this I'm living in the streets and starving to death, so the last thing I need today, right now, after the Working Lunch you created for all of us, is to have you start interrupting me like a scared little puppy in a big boy storm, whimpering and complaining. Grow up, right now, and leave me the fuck alone before you get me in trouble too and take me down with you. Learn to concentrate. I'm not going to lose my job because of Dan Kennard."

He put the earbud back in with an exasperated huff before Dan could think of a reply, and then he turned back to his computer again, twisting away from him like it was a formal and final dismissal, the official end of their conversation, and the funny thing was, that not only was it the end of their conversation, it would turn out to be the last time either of them spoke to each other ever again. In fact, by this point of the story many people were doing things for the last time without knowing it.

Over at Ken's apartment building, he was unlocking his front door while Kenndra waited behind him, growing chilly from the moisture and the gusts of wind I continued to side-arm between the buildings, which, along with the fact that their clothes were soaked through, would very soon create an awkward situation for them both.

As Ken jostled his key into his door, neither of them mentioned the softening concrete although they had both noticed it as they walked, feeling the suction of it with every step. There was a sinking feeling associated with it, and not just that they felt like if they didn't keep moving they would sink into it, but an emotional sinking too, a deep sense of dread as their minds recognized that it was not normal at all for concrete to soften during a rainstorm, but there it was, beginning to feel more and more like mud underneath their feet than concrete. To acknowledge something so obviously foreboding on what had otherwise, for them at least, been a pretty exciting day so far, would have broken the spell of burgeoning romance between them, which was another thing neither of them wanted to do.

Taking off their shoes inside the front door, it was impossible not to notice that they had disintegrated somewhat, just like the sidewalks and buildings were in the process of doing, so that there wasn't a whole lot left of them to take off. They seemed to fall apart in their hands like wet paper as they removed them, and the rubber soles had somehow become worn through during the short walk to Ken's apartment. Once removed, Ken went and pulled a couple of hand towels from a drawer next to the sink so they could dry themselves off, and he tossed one to Kenndra, who had taken a seat at the kitchen island.

"Make yourself at home," said Ken, getting straight to work opening a bottle of wine.

Kenndra looked around the apartment, a sense of calm coming over her followed by the strange sensation that she had been there before. Visually it was tidy: the counter was neatly organized, a coffee pot positioned next to the sink, a set of knives at the back of the counter, a set of four copper mugs hanging upside-down under one of the cabinets, the microwave gleaming above the stove, and a stylishly painted picture of a duck in sunglasses on the wall behind the sink. Then she realized why it all felt so familiar: everything down to the tiniest detail was exactly the same as it was in Dan's apartment, including the picture of the duck above the sink, except that it was all reversed; the layout of the kitchen and the rest of the rooms were set up in the exact mirror-image of Dan's apartment, just like Ken was the mirror image of Dan himself, except that now Dan had been totally replaced by Ken and all of Ken's stuff, which for Kenndra was like slipping into a parallel universe in which everything about her life had suddenly become fifteen percent better.

"I have the same picture of a duck above the sink in my apartment," she said, swiping the hand towel over her head and ruffling her hair with it. "Where did you get it?"

Ken was standing with his back to her pulling the corkscrew from the bottle of wine, and he paused to look at the picture. "I think I picked it up at one of those home goods stores after I moved in. I thought it was pretty cool, wearing the sunglasses and the bowtie and all. I don't know... something about it caught my eye."

"We probably got it from the same place," said Kenndra.

Whatever smile she had on her face vanished when she noticed the towel in her hand contained a whole handful of her hair, which had seemed to come out when she ruffled it and was now tangled up in the cloth. She gasped and stuffed the towel down between her legs just as Ken pulled the cork out with a pop. As he untwisted the cork from the corkscrew, he stopped and looked over his shoulder at her.

"Is everything okay?"

Kenndra composed herself quickly. "Yes, I'm fine. I just got the chills."

"Want me to turn the heat on for a few minutes?"

"No, no, I'm fine. It's okay. I'll warm up."

She looked at the towel again the way someone examines their own tissue as if to confirm what she had seen in it was real and not some kind of hallucination, and she saw again the matted clump of her own brown hair stuck to it.

"I need to use your bathroom," she said.

A few moments later, she was standing in the bathroom mirror and she saw with relief that it wasn't obvious which part of her head the hair had come from, the rest of her hair obscuring any visible bald spots. Looking herself over, considering any quick improvements she might make to her appearance before going back out to the kitchen, she happened to also notice that her blouse seemed to be dissolving in the same way her shoes had, the seams across the shoulders turning to mush and barely holding together, and it was apparent that it would soon cause her whole shirt to flop down, exposing her bra straps and her collarbone, but because her bra straps were also wet, it was only a matter of time before those fell apart too. She looked for a larger towel in the cabinet of the bathroom and found one in the exact same place they would have been at Dan's apartment, and she wrapped it around her shoulders thinking that surely his clothes would be dissolving too.

With one last look at herself in the mirror, fighting the instinct to try and fix her hair at all for fear it would cause even more of it to fall out, she walked back into the kitchen to find that Ken had poured them each a glass of wine and set out the cookies in the center of the island. As she approached the table again, it was easy to see that his shirt had dissolved into something more like a toga, revealing one of his sinewy shoulders underneath, and then she saw that his pants, like hers as well, would soon be nothing more than rags hanging from their waists. They realized that soon enough they would barely be clothed at all, my own little version of Adam and Eve at the end of the world, the two of them blushing at the awkwardness of the situation, all too aware of their impending nakedness.

"I'm not sure what's happening here," he said, referring to their clothes more than anything, but also referring to them too and the day they were having together. He looked down at himself. "But my clothes are falling apart."

"Mine too," she said, holding the towel tight around her shoulders. They stood facing each other silently for a few moments, eyeing each other cautiously, politely, trying not to stare but wanting to, while outside there was nothing but the sound of what they still assumed was rain coming down. The howling gusts of wind I was sending through caused the liquid to tinkle against the slowly dissolving apartment window glass, and I made the thunder rumble from the distance as the sounds of sirens continued to echo unbroken.

Finally Ken said, "I think we should change into some new clothes," and before they knew it I had steered them straight into Ken's bedroom.

Over at Klyber at around the same time, however, things weren't going as serendipitously for Dan. With under a half hour to go before they were allowed to leave for the evening, I poked out the glass in the window of Klyber's 33rd floor office, collapsing it from its window frame and sending the pieces scattering onto the office floor, but because everyone else was wearing their headphones and earbuds and were so locked into their work, they hadn't even noticed the window collapse, which meant that the responsibility to tell Lemming fell straight to Dan.

Instead of deliberately waiting for someone else to take up the responsibility of telling Lemming like he might have done in the past, he stood from his chair with resolve and looked around at his colleagues proudly, feeling like he owed them something after all he had put them through that day, his new, better self rising up within him, and he was suddenly unwilling to let the issue slide to someone else as he rushed towards Lemming's office. As he approached his door, he felt his forehead breakout in a sweat again at the prospect of going to his office uninvited, all of which could have been avoided had he not forgotten completely about the office Insta-Chat program they were supposed to use to communicate with each other.

Moments later, when Lemming saw Dan appear in his office doorway, with a tone of utter disgust and exasperation, he said, "You're turning into a fuckstick right before my eyes, Kennard. This is a blatant flouting of Klyber policy. Anything you need to tell me must be done through Insta-Chat and you know that. Don't be a piece of shit on purpose."

"Sir, I know we haven't had a good day—"

"—That's an understatement, Kennard. Get to your point," he snapped.

"The office window that I was looking out of earlier has shattered to pieces, sir. The carpet is flooding now too because of the rain coming in, and I thought you would want to know right away."

"How in the hell did that happen?" said Lemming furiously, practically ejecting himself from his desk chair. Dan stepped back. "What did you do now?"

"Me? Nothing. I was working, but since I forgot my earbuds today at home, I heard it crash."

"Forgot your earbuds, huh? No wonder you can't

focus."

"Perhaps, but I won't forget them ever again, Mr. Lemming. The window though, it just happened a minute ago. It's already soaking the floor."

"I still don't see why this couldn't have been communicated through Insta-Chat. Do you think that you can run here faster than an electronic message?"

"This seemed like a special circumstance, sir. I thought I should tell you in person. Water is pouring in now, soaking the carpet."

"You thought wrong, Kennard. We invested in Insta-Chat for a reason and we expect you to use it. Besides, did you think I wouldn't find out about the window myself during my evening inspections?" he said, surprisingly diminishing the importance of the window.

"I didn't know you conducted evening inspections, sir. It's just that water is—"

"—Enough about the water pouring in, you've said that already. Twice. Now go back to your desk, enjoy the fresh air, lord knows we need it up here with the ventilation system we have, and I will address the matter of the window during my evening inspections. A broken window can be replaced, Kennard, wasted time cannot. Now, go!" he huffed. "Time is of the essence, Kennard! Don't you get that?"

Dan rushed back to his cubicle and sat back down in his desk chair, saw that the sandwich box next to his monitor seemed to be melting under its own meager weight, the edges collapsing apart despite the fact that he hadn't touched it since lunchtime, and then he felt his stomach grumble, needy at the sight of food and pleading with him to eat something, anything. His tried to focus on his computer screen, but it was beginning to blur his eyes and cause him to feel dizzy, so he decided just to sit there meditatively and wait for the clock to tick down on the end of his day, preparing himself for the journey home where he could finally eat and lie down to rest.

He spent his last few minutes of work in something of a trance, staring towards the window and the dark brown rectangle of sky beyond it, looking at the glass spread out on the thin gray industrial carpet floor, which was turning darker as it became wetter, expanding outward in a dark gray semi-circle. Outside, I made the wind whistle and the thunder rumble while I thought about how much more I wanted to put everyone through.

He snapped out of it when he saw his colleagues around him were shutting down their computers and removing their headphones and earbuds for the day, straightening up their desks, and he realized with tremendous relief that it was finally time to go. As everyone gathered their things and rose from their desks in near unison, someone on the other side of the office said, "Hey, what happened to the window?" and as everyone turned to look, another person said, "Has anyone told Lemming?" and then Gary, after sneering at the broken window like it was an injured animal that had to be left behind, said "He'll find out during his evening inspections," and they all shuffled out together towards the building elevators.

Across the city at about the same time, Kenndra was drinking expensive red wine and eating soft-baked chocolate chip cookies in Ken's bed, wearing one of his over-sized t-shirts and a pair of his mesh gym shorts, admiring how much nicer Ken's bed was compared to the one Dan had in his apartment.

Kenndra, in answer to the question her mother always asked her to consider about the men she dated, felt like even though it had only been a few hours, she could finally answer with a resounding "Yes! Yes!" inside her mind, something that she could never say so resoundingly about Dan, and from then on, it was hard for her to contain her excitement that she had finally, at long last, come upon the One. She felt it right away.

Without me making things go exactly as they did, they would have just been two people stopped at the same red light, which on any other day would have turned green and sent them on with the rest of their lives, never to see each other again. But as we all know, this was a special day, in so, so many ways, and not only for them, but for everyone involved, including me.

For the rest of the night, I put Ken and Kenndra close together in Ken's king-sized bed, allowing them the grace of spending the remainder of their first and last evening together on top of and then underneath Ken's luxurious red sheets, flirting and talking as if they had known each other for years and years, drinking the red wine and eating the cookies from the red box, accents of red planted everywhere in the background by me as a symbol of their ill-fated love and impending deaths.

As we prepare to read our last sentences about them together, I would like to take a few words to reassure you that their relationship would end as well it could have for them and that I gave them both the best ending I could. At one point they would open a second bottle of wine, and then later, after the most romantic and passionate sex of their mutual lives, they would both fall asleep for the last time, their naked bodies entwined skin-to-skin until at last they too were absorbed back into the prelapsarian ether together under the weight of the apartment building as I sent it collapsing to the ground later that night.

Well before all of that would happen though, on the other side of Sunset City, Dan was still pushing his way out through the lobby of his office building thinking only of the food he could eat when he got home before he too collapsed into himself like the window had or like the world at large was in the process of doing.

Like him, everyone else was struggling their way to the exit too, eager to go wherever it was they all planned to go after work. For Gary, it was the The Quack House Bar & Grill where he intended to drink several beers in a row, while Denise or Debbie or whatever the hell her name was intended to go straight home so that she could watch the nightly news with her husband and prepare dinner. Of course, it shouldn't be totally unexpected that I would make Lemming unique in all of this, not having given him any loved ones to go see and not making him feel particularly hungry at this point of the story either. Besides that, as a rule of character, he wouldn't be able to leave without doing his evening inspections anyway, and as a result, while everyone else in the office was leaving, Lemming was consulting the Klyber Handbook regarding the window, where he would soon discover that according to Executive Tower protocol "a broken window on any floor above the third needed to be replaced immediately" or, to summarize a bit, Klyber could end up in a real legal tangle should one of his more clever employees confront him about it. This fact of circumstance would lead to Lemming going on to spend the entirety of his last night as a character attempting to have the window replaced in an office that, funny enough, wasn't going to be an office much longer anyway, not to mention attending to all of the associated paperwork that would never be sent, and all before the next day that would never come! Everyone else funneling their way towards the exit doors at the end of the workday no doubt had their own private lives to try and finish out too that night, which I shudder to even try and articulate for you.

Downstairs, Dan had finally emerged onto the mushy, mud-like sidewalks and stepped out into the falling liquid for the first time since that morning, regarding it all with wonder. He soon broke loose from the mass of people and began walking back in the same direction he came from that morning, but the sidewalks had already been reduced to nothing more than a muddy gray path between teetering buildings while the sky, vicious and dark, loomed above everything.

He trudged his way to the intersection he had crossed earlier, crossed back again, and made his way down the sidewalk like he did every day after work. He passed the trashcan on the corner where all this started, and he noticed that it had taken on the shape of a crumpled soda can, and I sent him a flickering memory from that morning, from when he missed it with his candy wrapper—I made him picture the wrapper fluttering away on a gust of my strong wind, made him feel the same pang of regret again in a flash as he wondered for the briefest of moments where it might have ended up landing—but he was far too hungry to linger on it.

He made his way up to his second-story apartment a few minutes later, opened the door, and immediately went to the kitchen island to make the sandwich and eat the chips. He made one sandwich and ate it so fast that he immediately made another one. It was right around that moment when I toppled my first building, starting from the outside of the city and advancing in a spiral domino effect that would soon end where it started, with Dan Kennard at the center. The toppling buildings sent shockwaves resounding up through the muck and his own building and through the worn, disintegrating soles of Dan's shoes as he stood in his kitchen, staring absently at the painting of the duck above the sink. But with food finally in his stomach, his awareness of himself and his surroundings returned to him, and he noticed finally, that his clothes were disintegrating, turning to mush against his skin, akin to wet tissue on his body.

Meanwhile, Gary would make it to the Quack House like he always did after work, but like everyone else who had been exposed to the falling liquid, he wouldn't be very far into his second beer when he too would notice that his clothes were turning into mush along with everything else. While Gary was realizing he might soon be drinking naked in public, up on the thirty-third floor of the Klyber offices, Lemming was realizing with some overdue alarm that the thin industrial carpet by the broken window was seemingly disappearing before his eyes wherever it had gotten wet, slowly revealing the white concrete underneath, which upon even closer inspection he saw was becoming soft on top, like icing on a cake, a fact he discovered when he pressed a finger into it and scooped some up with his fingertip. Debbie or Debra or Denise or whatever the hell her name was never made it home to her husband that night because of the permanent red lights throughout the city but also because the roads had become impassable and soon enough the effects of the rain meant I didn't have to do anything anymore but let the buildings topple themselves.

For Dan, who was changing into his pajamas in his bedroom as all of this was happening around him, as the central character of this novella it's natural that his building would be the very last to fall. He spent the night tossing and turning while the city toppled around him, all which produced sounds and sensations that he continued to mistake for thunder even though it was more like a continuous earthquake, an extended rumbling he could feel vibrating his couch and rattling the various trinkets and small pictures Kenndra had decorated his apartment with, even causing the painting of the duck above his sink to tilt slightly. He kept himself awake hopelessly dreaming that

Kenndra would come home from wherever she was, drifting in-and-out of sleep until at some point his alarm went off and it was the morning again.

When he sat up on his couch on that last morning of his existence, he was eager to get to work on time and prove to himself and his colleagues and Lemming that he was a changed man, ready to embrace the Klyber lifestyle. He was going to model himself after Gary from then on, and as he rubbed his eyes and stretched, perched on the edge of his couch, he was struck by the overwhelming stillness of the world.

The bright white light coming in through the half-closed blinds of every window of his apartment was understood by Dan initially as a sign that the weather had cleared, that the storm had passed, that one of the strangest days he could ever remember had finally come to an end and he could start anew again. He checked his phone for a message from Kenndra, but he found nothing. He decided to call her, alarmed that she had never come home, but it went straight to voicemail, so he left a message for her, hoping she was okay, and asking if she would please call him as soon as she could because he was worried about her, and then he said that he loved her, and he said it was something he knew he didn't say to her enough, but for some reason he felt compelled to say to her that morning. He said it again one more time before he hung up, his last words to her.

When Dan emerged from his apartment building after getting dressed, it was like opening the door to another planet. There were no more sirens and the bright white light of the sky enveloped everything like a fog so that it felt like he could hardly see more than ten feet in front of himself when in fact he was actually seeing everything there ever was. He descended the still-standing concrete stairs cautiously, finding them soft and gooey under his feet like he remembered the sidewalks being the night before and which dispelled any notion he might have maintained that it was all just a dream.

As he stepped onto the sidewalk, Dan stopped to look back at his building from which no one else had emerged nor would emerge but him, the anonymous masses dissolved from the story overnight like nearly everything else, and from somewhere deep inside of it there came the sudden rumble of final collapse. Dan backpedaled away from it, taking cover behind the rubble across the street, and then watched in awe as I slowly smushed his own building beneath my godly thumb.

When Dan got the sense that I was done, he rose up from behind the pile he was hiding behind, pulled his phone from his pocket to check the time, and then hurried off in the direction of an office building that no longer existed, running late again as usual, running towards me and the glowing edge of my creation where he would soon blink out of existence along with everything else, disappearing into the void of my blinking cursor forever.

Kennardo Kills Dan Twice

As any of my friends would tell you, I loved that goldfish. I would post selfies with the two of us online sometimes, me holding the fish jar up next to my face, grinning happily into the camera. Every time I posted a photo, I got a lot of thumbs-ups from my friends and a bunch of comments saying how "awesome" the goldfish was, and how "cool" I was for having a pet goldfish at all at my age, which was thirty-nine.

I'm able to give my own thumbs-ups to their comments, so I do. One time, someone asked me where I got the goldfish, and I typed: "Pet Wise." They thumbsed that up almost immediately for going to Pet Wise, which made me feel good because I had almost gone to Pet Depot! Can you imagine the kind of goldfish they sell at that place? At a Depot? All the thumbs-ups I would have lost? I didn't want to think about it. Someone else asked me what my goldfish's name was, and I typed back: "Dan." They thumbsed that up right away and several other friends of mine too, so I knew they liked the name.

Another person asked: "Is that just a large glass pickle jar it's living in?!?!" and I typed back: "Herman's! The best!" and they thumbsed that up too.

We fell into a routine, me and that goldfish: I kept Dan on my nightstand, right next to my smartphone, a box of tissues, and a small beside lamp. In the morning I would carry him with me into the bathroom and tell him what I had planned for my day as I splashed water on my face or shaved or even while I was showering, trying to tell him about the real world outside of his Herman's fish jar. At night, maybe during dinner or while watching television, I would tell him about how my day went, relative to what I had said in the morning, and I could tell sometimes by the way he swam around the jar that he understood what I was getting at. I truly believe that he understood me. Like when I talked about how I hated my job sometimes, he would swim straight into the glass and stay there, his nose pressed against it and his tail flipping quickly, as if he was trying to swim through the glass and get out, and I thought: Yes! That's how it feels at work! You're a genius, Dan! and I would clap at his imitation of my life and we would have a laugh. It went along like that for almost eight months, me and Dan and the Herman's pickle jar and the selfies and the thumbs-ups, and all I can do now is look back and think: Man, those were the days.

The day Dan went belly-up I immediately posted it online to my friends. I typed that I was sad to the same degree anyone can be sad about losing someone they loved, even though it was only a goldfish, which was a message that got a lot of thumbs-ups. My thinking was, why should we, as people, not mourn the life of every creature that passes before us, even some of the bugs? Why unnecessarily crush and kill bugs if you could save them, usher them back outside on a piece of computer paper or inside a glass jar? I typed that online and that got some thumbs-ups, too.

By nighttime I was sitting in my recliner, making my way through a six-pack of beer with the television on in front of me, but I was still thinking about Dan too. I couldn't shake the image from my mind of watching his little orange body swirl in the toilet water, spinning downwards towards the bottom until he disappeared forever with the last rush of water. Then to hear the toilet gurgle once and for all, the water gone, I knew that was it. "Bye, bye, Dan," I said, and I clapped at his life, slowly and sadly.

I felt my heart shift as I stared down into the toilet, watching it slowly fill up again. The entire house was silent except for the toilet water running, and after that I entered a terrible circle of emotional pain. I wanted to talk to Dan about his own death so that I could feel better, but of course by then Dan was in the bowels of my septic system somewhere, floating with the feces or whatever. Sitting back in my recliner later on, I was trying not to think about it anymore, so I drank. It was at that moment, drinking, staring at the television without really watching it, that I noticed him coming up my driveway.

I caught his movement out of the corner of my eye through the half-opened blinds next to me, and I sat up to get a better view. Sure enough, there was a man coming up my driveway with a white face and a red nose, a brown hat tipped back on his forehead. He appeared exhausted, stagger-walking towards my front porch in an over-sized brown suit, his pant legs wet and dirty near the ankles because it had rained earlier and they had been dragging under his heels.

I went over to my front door and watched him through the peephole as he came the rest of the way, but as he went up the two steps of my front porch, the tip of one of his long red shoes must have clipped the top step because next thing I knew he stumbled hard into the back wall of my porch, shoulder-first, rattling the whole house. If I had been sleeping, surely the sound of his fall would have startled me awake. I watched him pull himself to his feet with a grimace and brush himself off, clutching his shoulder, wincing as he began wind-milling his arm to loosen it up, moving towards my front door.

He put one eye up to the peephole first, pretending like he could see through from outside or something, cupping his hands around his face to pretend to see better, and for a few moments I felt like we were sharing the same eye. Then he backed up, coughed hard into his fist, seemed to try and compose himself, and then reached out and knocked on my door.

"Who are you? What are you doing here?" I said through the door.

Through the peephole, I watched him point at himself, a surprised look on his face as if I should have known who he was all along, and then he held up a finger indicating I needed to wait just a second, and then, smiling as he did it, I watched him remove a large plastic bag of water from inside his coat and raise it up for me to see. It was a grand gesture, the way he did it, like the conclusion of a magic trick, a big reveal, which in some way it was, but I was astonished to discover that inside that bag of water was an orange goldfish, swimming and twitching with life just like old Dan used to do!

I opened the door, and in my excitement I never once considered whether that was the same Dan the Goldfish, or how he knew about Dan the Goldfish at all, or even why someone would be carrying a goldfish around inside their jacket in the first place, but as I stepped through the door to greet the man and thank him for returning my goldfish to life, which is how it felt even if deep down I knew it wasn't Dan, he stepped aside cruelly and tossed the bag high into the air towards my front lawn. I followed its course with my eyes—its silhouette crossing in front of the moon briefly—and then I heard it plop somewhere in the grass.

"Dan!" I shrieked.

I leapt off the porch, almost tripping over his extra-long shoes, and hurried into my front yard where the ground was squishy and wet underneath my feet from all the rain we'd had lately. I scanned the darkness, fearing the worst the whole time, wondering how well the bag was tied or if my grass was spiky enough to pierce the plastic and pop it. I imagined Dan flopping helplessly as the water drained away into the lawn, and I wondered if there would be time enough to get him back inside and save him if that's what it came down to. I prepared myself for the worst, but I didn't think I could bear losing two goldfish in one night, even if it wasn't the same goldfish.

I scanned the yard, and I could feel my heart racing as I took another cautious step forward, scanning all the time with wide eyes, and then the worst thing happened—I stepped onto the bag with the tip of my shoe, exploding it all over the place. It was too dark out to see where the goldfish could have exploded too, but right away I dropped to my knees and began fingering through the grass anyway, trying to feel for his tiny, quivering body. My own body blocked what light there was coming from the porch and it felt like I was searching the inside of my own shadow.

I turned back to the clown, but he was already gone. I wanted to ask him why he did that, why he threw the goldfish into the lawn instead of giving it to me. Some people are just mean, I figured, and some people just like to be mean to others as some demented form of personal entertainment, and that's all this clown was looking for I guess.

I looked around to try and spot him walking away and I listened for the sound of slapping footsteps on pavement, but all I heard was the muffled sounds of my neighbors across the street, laughing at something on television, and it felt like they were laughing at me, laughing at the thirty-nine year old man on his knees in his front lawn, crying over the death of a fifty-cent goldfish all over again—so you might see now why I don't have too many kind words about this Kennardo character.

Waiting for Kennard

It became clear soon enough that my colleagues were losing patience with me, especially once they realized that I was only interested in discussing Kennard and it had nothing to do with the usual business. I looked at everyone around the table, picking at their fingernails, checking their watches, no doubt anxious about their dropping Efficiency Ratios, thinking about what other, more productive things they could be doing at the moment instead of being in this conference room with me.

"It's very important to me that I am as precise as possible about all this. I'm developing a theory regarding my relationship with Kennard—all of our relationships with Kennard—"

"—Don't bring me into this," blurted Diane. "He means nothing to me. He's a non-entity."

"Diane, first of all, come on, you're already involved. Trust me. We all are. This is just the beginning. He's manipulating all of us at the same time, and I think you'll see that it's quite incredible when you understand what I'm getting at here. Granted, so far you're all just side characters, so perhaps that's why you don't care as much as I do as the protagonist, but—"

Gary cut me off, "—Wait, wait, wait," he began. "Are you serious right now?" He laughed and looked at everyone else, the annoyed tension that had been mounting in the room dissipating in an instant.

"I have proof," I said. "He's been leaving me notes."

"Wait. Who has?" said Scott.

"Kennard."

Scott looked around the conference room like he wasn't sure where he was anymore, like he had appeared there against his will (which, according to my theory, would have been true— for me and for everyone else sitting around the table impatiently) and then he said, "What the fuck is going on?"

"No one knows what you're fucking talking about, Dan." That was Nancy from a few chairs down, chewing her gum with an open mouth in a way that drove me crazy.

I pulled a wad of sticky-note papers from inside my sportcoat as a way to try and prove I was serious—little notes from Kennard that had been collected over the past few days that I had begun finding taped to doors and furniture, always coming upon them with a shock. If I am the protagonist of this novel, I can't say I'm finding it very enjoyable so far, to know so little of what's going on yet so compelled to keep going. Needless to say, I now carried these notes around with me everywhere. I tossed them confidently into the center of the table as evidence of our collective situation.

"There they are. It's been four days since the first one appeared."

Scott snatched the wad of notes and pulled them apart

curiously, reading them with a sniffling condescension. In my head, I told myself it wasn't his fault he acted that way, it was only Kennard making him do it.

"I want to bash my head in listening to this," said Gary.

"Can we go yet?" said Nancy. "My E-Ratios and DST numbers have dipped over the last month with me getting sick and all, so I can't sit here and talk about this Kennard person anymore."

"Me neither," said Gary. "I second all of that."

"Me three," said Diane.

"What do you think of the notes?" I asked Scott. "I've started to number them."

"This is meaningless drivel. Verbal excrement that could have been written by anybody," he said, tossing the papers back into the center of the table again like he was flinging slop from his fingers. He rose from his seat, triggering the other three to gather their things and stand too, and then out they went, fairly pissed.

Diane paused in the doorway, last to leave, and said, "It sounds like someone is playing a joke on you, Dan."

I let out an exhausted sigh. "I wish that were true, Diane, I really do. But if there is a joke here, it's on all of us."

I discovered the first note a couple days before I called the meeting with everyone at work. It was addressed to me directly, and I found it taped to the coffeemaker on my kitchen counter one morning while I was getting ready for work. It said, "Dan, I thought I should tell you that you are the protagonist of my newest novel, *No Turning* Back, and while the coffee you are about to make may seem real, it is only a detail in a sentence created by me, your author," and then it was signed "Kennard."

I snatched it off the coffeemaker and brought it to show

Layla, my girlfriend, who was still lying in bed. She had the sheets positioned so that they barely covered her chest, and she looked incredibly beautiful there looking at me, sitting up against the headboard, the sun outside having just broken through the bottom of the window, a little ribbon of pink under the black shadow rectangle of the curtain.

"What is this?" I said, holding it out to her.

"What is what?"

"This note from Kennard. I found it on the coffee machine."

"Who is Kennard?"

"I don't know. Apparently he's an author of some kind."

"What does it say?"

I handed her the letter to read herself. "It says I am the protagonist of his new novel, *No Turning Back*."

"You? A protagonist?" she said, raising an eyebrow.

"Yeah. It's addressed to me. Why can't I be a protagonist?"

"If you're the protagonist, then what am I?"

"I don't know. It doesn't say."

"Hmm."

"You're my girlfriend I guess."

We looked at each other blankly, neither of us sure what to say next while Kennard twiddled his thumbs somewhere.

On my drive home from work the afternoon of my meeting, I navigated my way back to my apartment again like I did every day, the passing scenery of billboards, industrial plants, and shopping centers managing to distract me temporarily from my thoughts of Kennard, but as I neared my complex, I turned to thinking of what dinner he would have me order and picturing the scotch he would have me pour myself as soon as I walked in. I wondered what kind of night he had in mind for me. In fact, ever since I realized that I was the central figure of this story, I became helplessly preoccupied with wondering what he was going to do to me next.

When I got back to my apartment that evening, I found another note taped to my apartment door that said, "When I got back to my apartment that evening, I found another note taped to my apartment door," and I laughed uncomfortably to myself because I wasn't sure what came first, me thinking it or me reading it. He didn't sign his name at the end of this one like he did with the others and it was the shortest note yet, but I knew it was him again. I looked up at the ceiling helplessly, which was where I assumed he was always looking in from, watching me and everyone else from above somewhere.

The next thing I knew Layla pulled the door open from inside, and the note I had been staring at went gliding away from me, the edges fluttering in the vacuum of air she created as she pulled the door open, seeming to expect me at just that moment. She seemed as glad to have me home again as I was to be there, which gave me a nice feeling. One thing I can say about Kennard is that in pairing me with Layla he has at least provided me with one happy, positive person to share scenes with. She's on my side, unlike most of the people I work with who are perpetually miserable and annoyed.

"Kennard left me another note," I said.

"Another one? How many is that now?"

"This is the fifth one."

I slipped past her and she snatched the note from the door as if she had spent the whole day practicing to do it then sat down at the kitchen table, reading it herself. I went and poured myself a drink at the counter, surprised that Kennard allowed me to fill my glass so high. Sometimes I fear he has made me into an alcoholic if only because he can't think of anything else to have me be doing when I sit down to talk with people. I sat down across from Layla with my drink and she put the note in the middle of the table under the full glare of the overhead kitchen lamp hanging over us.

The two of us stared at it together for a while in silence. I sipped occasionally from my drink. Eventually, I took the others from inside my jacket pocket and tossed them into the center of the table to go with it.

"This won't help prove anything," she said finally.

"I know. You should have seen me at the meeting earlier. Scott read some of them and said it was meaningless drivel; verbal excrement. I'm nervous for him, honestly. I mean, he's a character too, and to be so harsh to the person who is responsible for his well-being isn't a great idea, right?"

"Maybe Kennard has a sense of humor. He's using Scott to make fun of himself."

"Convincing the others of all this is going to be harder than we thought," I mused.

"It will be as hard or as easy as Kennard makes it," said Layla calmly.

I took another sip from my drink and looked up into the light hanging over our kitchen table where I imagined Kennard to be watching us from, his world just on the other side of it, deciding at his keyboard what to do with us next, and I found myself wondering how many pages he planned to fill. I sipped long from my scotch again, held it in my mouth, let it burn the back of my tongue and throat before I swallowed it in a gulp. We sat silently regarding the situation we had suddenly found ourselves in.

"I got the most tortuous email today from this Gavin

guy in the Outer Office," I blurted. "He's new, but it was so long that it really sank my Daily Efficiency Ratio. I had to read it twice to get it. I shouldn't have to read it twice to get it, you know? I hate that."

"Tortuous? What does that mean?"

I watched myself pause, unable to bring a definition immediately to mind, suddenly wondering what I might say next. "I don't know. Kennard must be putting words into my mouth."

"He's putting words into all our mouth's, Dan. How else would you explain someone using words they don't know?"

"I don't know."

"You could start paying attention to how they speak and call them out when they say certain things."

"That feels like too much work." I drank some more. "Besides, isn't this all up to him?"

"I wish Kennard would just come right out and reveal himself to everyone."

"You mean like write himself in?"

"Yeah. Stop all this fooling around. Introduce himself to us."

"I guess we'll find out, right?"

The next morning Kennard had us all back at work again and I found myself talking to Gary, whose cubicle is next to mine. Somehow, I had already initiated a conversation about Kennard and we were right in the middle of it.

"If we're just characters in a novel, then who am I talking to right now?" he asked me.

I thought about it. "Kennard, I guess."

"Who are *you* talking to?" he asked.

"We're all Kennard here. That's what I'm trying to

explain."

"So Kennard is just talking to himself through us?"

"What else is writing to you?" I retorted.

"You sound insane. You know that, right?"

"It's Kennard. I don't have any control over this. Kennard is making me sound insane."

"Here's a question for you: Why are you trying to convince us all that we're characters in your story? What's the point? If we believe you or if we don't, who cares?"

"All I know is that it's what Kennard has given me to do. I suppose I figured you would all want to know."

"Well I don't. I don't want to know. Kennard hasn't made me want to know. Maybe he should leave the rest of us a note too once in a while if he wants us all to know about the true nature of our existence."

"Would you believe it if you got a note?"

"No. I would think it was someone playing a joke on me. There's no such person as Kennard. He doesn't exist."

"So you think all the notes I'm finding are a joke too?"

"Yeah, actually, I do. I do think it's all a big joke."

"Well that feels like a big mistake. I'm nervous for you. I'm nervous for Scott too. You're both a little too dismissive of the one person who is in charge of all this. It's blasphemy!"

I looked around at the office and for the first time I can remember it felt more like a set, like I was sitting on a stage and somewhere far off people were watching us perform this scene for them.

I was thinking of you out there.

"Are we done with this yet?" he said. "All we ever do lately is talk about Kennard. I have actual work to do and so do you."

"Fine."

"And by the way, I would be more nervous for you than us. If you're the protagonist like you think you are, doesn't the worst stuff usually happen to them?"

He turned back to his desk and left me frozen there, thinking that he was probably right, thinking that perhaps he was only Kennard dressed up like Gary and that he was trying to prepare me for everything that he was about to do to me, and I began to wonder what sort of story I was caught up in.

In the bathroom later on, I had only just begun toilet-papering the seat when he appeared noiselessly in the stall next to me as if he had simply been farted into existence on the other side of the thin metal wall that separated us. I froze in my stall for a moment like some innocent fawn upon a distant gunshot, and then, with the pressure building, I snapped another short piece of toilet paper from the roll and placed it across the back of the seat.

I bent down quickly to glance at his shoes and found them to be pointing toes-to-bowl, and my heart fluttered with the hope that maybe he was only in there to pee and I would soon be left to myself again because I think there's one activity that we can all agree is best done in private, an activity which I really badly needed to get on with at that moment, but which, because of his presence, I would not be able to bring myself to do. My hopes rested precariously on the knowledge that, for reasons that have never been clear to me, some men prefer to pee in a stall as opposed to a urinal, and so I waited anxiously in the hopes that this mysterious man was one of those kinds of men. While I waited, I finished papering my seat, snapping off one more short piece and placing it on the right side, making sure to be loud enough to make it clear I was there first, my seat already papered-up, and if anyone should consider leaving it should be him, not me.

I unbuckled my pants defiantly in preparation to sit down, and then my heart just about broke at the sound of his plastic toilet paper holder rumbling from the other side of the wall—his side—as it was spun, followed by the sharp snapping off of his own strips of toilet paper. With my belt buckle dangling open at the top of my pants, I considered briefly the idea of sliding all of my toilet paper into the toilet, "packing up shop" so to speak, deferring to him for now and trying again in a few minutes so that I might be alone, but it was almost like it was too late. My body sensed that I was near a toilet and in this particular instance, with the pressure building even further along my beltline, I realized that on this day, unlike days in the past, there would be no turning back this time.

On a different day, I probably would have left—I've done that plenty of times before—but the fact that I didn't (couldn't is more like it!) is a testament to how badly I needed to get on with it. I remember telling myself, "Fuck it," before unzipping my fly all the way down, and then I lowered myself onto the toilet seat, careful all the while not to let my cell phone slide out of my back pocket and into the toilet water or tumbling down onto the horrendous-looking tooth-colored tile of the bathroom floor.

I couldn't help thinking that if I were alone, this is the part where the moment of relief would come sweeping over me, but with this man in the stall next to me, sometime during the act of sitting down I was unable to bring myself to let it go, and so I ended up just sitting there, clenching impatiently, my elbows pressing into my bare thighs as I stared down into the crotch of my underwear, stretched out between my ankles.

I listened to the man in the stall next to me snap off the

rest of his toilet paper and presumably lay it down on his own seat just like I had done on mine moments earlier, and in that moment, before things got too far along, I was tempted to speak out to him, to ask him to leave, to come back later if he could so that I might get on with it, me being first and all, but of course I didn't say a word not only because it isn't customary to speak to another man while you're each doing what we were both readying ourselves to do, but also because I'm a coward when it comes to confronting other people. All my life it's been a point of weakness for me, especially at work and even more especially because I owed so many people so much money that through the years I had become afraid to say anything that might be misconstrued as disagreeable.

So in my own self-made fashion, I suffered my fate silently in my own stall, leaning forward to look at his feet again just in time to see the man's black shoes start pivoting with the jagged pirouetting of a car making a k-turn on a narrow street (the stalls being quite cramped and narrow in this particular bathroom) until he finally positioned himself heel-to-bowl and sat down with a groan.

I was holding out hope that this man had no scruples about what we were there to do— unlike me, who had *lots* of scruples about all kinds of things, but especially about this— and that soon enough he would just go ahead and do it already. My plan was to wait him out so that I could be alone and at peace, but that's not what happened. Instead, as I continued scrolling the news on my phone, half-reading, half-reluctantly-listening for progress from the other side of the stall wall, after a minute or two it became apparent that this other man seemed to be doing the exact same thing that I was doing, which was sit-holding it all in, each of us waiting impatiently for the other one to go first.

It was ludicrous.

I imagined him sitting there on the other side of the wall in the same position as me, a mirror image of myself, scrolling on his own phone probably, leaning forward with his elbows on his bare thighs just like I was doing, waiting instead for *me* to go ahead and get on with it. The recognition of our emerging standoff created a real panic in me so that there was suddenly just as much pressure above to find some way out as there was below, my mind reeling in search of some solution to the terrifying awkwardness of having to shit mere feet from someone else.

In the moment, I became transcendently aware of my apparent human-ness, the consequences of every sound fully known, but it was the silence that confirmed my greatest fears because for the longest time, for what felt like several minutes at least but was probably only seconds, there were no sounds at all, and then the man on the other side cleared his throat as if to speak.

"Dan, we need to talk," he said.

"Are you talking to me? Who are you?"

Both of us spoke in a clenched sort of way, like we were straining to hold a great weight.

"Haven't you been getting my notes?"

"Kennard?" I said. "Is that you? What are you doing here?"

"I wrote myself in to talk to you. I'm afraid there's been a mistake."

"A mistake?" I said through clenched teeth.

"This isn't a novel anymore. It's a short story."

"Okay…"

"And I'm sorry to say this, but it's almost the end now."

"What about the beginning and the middle?"

"I find more and more that I can only write endings these days. Have you ever seen a child's kite take flight before quickly spiking itself into the ground?"

"Yeah?"

"That's kind of how I write now."

"Oh," I said. "So what's next?"

"That's what I'm trying to figure out."

"I'd prefer a happy ending if that's possible."

"No promises," he said, and then he broke the standoff with a grunt followed by what sounded like a bag of apples being poured into a bucket of water. He finished up soon after that and then I took my turn, trying to be quick so that I might be able to catch him in person before he wrote himself back out again.

When I returned to my desk from the bathroom, I found a note stuck to my computer monitor that said, "Here goes nothing!"

I turned to Gary and said, "Where did this note come from?"

"Someone came by and stuck it to your monitor," he said, chewing a granola bar like a fucking cow.

"Who?"

"I don't know. He didn't say and I didn't ask."

"I want to strangle you right now, Gary. Do you get that? Is he still here?"

"I don't know."

"What did he look like? Do you remember?"

"It feels like an eternity ago," he said lazily. "He had a beard I think. Small gap in his front teeth. I never saw him before. He looked a lot like you, actually." He finally swallowed the granola bar he had been chewing.

I snatched the note from my screen and held it out to

him so he could read it. "It's another note from Kennard."

"'Here goes nothing!'? What does that mean?"

"He met me in the bathroom just now and told me the end is near. He only writes endings apparently. It sounds like he's about to put an end to us any minute now."

"Does that include me?"

"I would guess so. We're all in this together. Diane, Scott, you, me, Lemming."

"So it's almost over?"

"Yes." I stood up and looked around the office. "How long ago did he stick this on my monitor?"

"I don't know. Right before you came back."

"He could still be here!"

I raised my head above the thicket of cubicles that filled our office area and scanned for a man with a beard, but I saw nothing except the backs of my colleagues between me and the farthest walls of our office, hunched over and clattering away at their keyboards like I was supposed to be doing. Then, on the edge of my periphery, I saw motion near the stairwell and watched as the back of a man in a navy blue suit slipped through the metal door and disappeared from sight, and before I knew what I was doing, I took off after him, efficiency ratios and DST numbers be damned.

Seconds later, I pushed my way through the same door and into the same concrete stairwell that I had watched him enter just moments before, hoping to catch a better glimpse of him, hoping to talk to him about what he planned on doing to me now that the end was near so that I could at least prepare myself. I leaned over the rail and looked down, listening for the sounds of footsteps below, searching for his hand spiraling downward on a rail beneath me, but instead found nothing but silence.

My boss Lemming approached me as soon as I came in from the stairwell, his hair slickly parted to the side, his gold-circle glasses pushed firmly back on the bridge of his nose so that it looked like he was pressing his face against a window. He was holding some papers in his hand, presumably to give to me.

"Where the hell were you? I've been looking all over for you?"

"I was on the stairwell, sir."

"For ten minutes? I've literally been standing at your desk for the last ten minutes. Gary said you would be right back."

"Ten-minutes?" I said doubtfully. I checked my watch and sure enough ten minutes had passed somehow.

"I don't appreciate having my time wasted, Dan."

"I'm sorry, sir. I don't know what happened. I felt like I was only out there for a few seconds. He must have used a space break to fuck with me."

"He who? What are you talking about?"

"Kennard. I spoke to him while we were using the restroom, but I have more questions. He left me a note on his way out and I thought I saw him go through this door into the stairwell. That's why I was out there."

"Kennard, huh?" Lemming stared at me with a grave look in his eyes. "Come into my office for a minute, we need to talk."

I followed him down a short hallway to his office and sat across from him thinking this would be it; this was the end coming right now. My efficiency ratios and DST numbers had plummeted over the last few days as I became preoccupied with the notes and the meaning and the anticipation of it all, so Lemming would probably be within his rights to fire me if he wanted.

The lighting in his office was dim, the overhead fluorescents turned off in lieu of a corner light that cast long shadows over everything. Lemming's face was cast in a semi-darkness, his eyes translucent. I adjusted my blazer in my seat, pulling the front closed in an effort to straighten myself out and appear presentable even though my mind was beginning to spin.

It was hard not to notice that my chair was several inches lower than his chair on the other side of his large, glossy desk, scattered with papers, and I could feel him looking down on me, the whole arrangement an obvious setup designed to reflect the power imbalance between me and the entire world Kennard was creating for me, line by line. I leaned forward in the chair, leaning upwards towards Lemming who seemed to loom over me like a dark cloud. It seemed to me that Kennard was laying it on pretty thick, wherever he was writing this from. Lemming laid down the papers he had been holding on the desk in front of him, running his hands over them to flatten them out and then he cleared his throat to speak.

"Tell me about this Kennard person," he said.

"You'll never believe me when I say it, but he is an author."

"An author?"

"He writes fiction."

"Okay." His brow rose skeptically as he waited for me to keep going.

"As it happens, he has been leaving me notes the last several days and just now he wrote himself in to tell me that the end is near."

"He told you all this in the bathroom just now?"

"Yes."

"The end of what?"

"This story that we're all in. He's the author, and he's about to end it. He wanted me to know."

"What about the beginning and the middle?"

"I asked him that too. He doesn't write those parts anymore. He only writes endings."

"Well it sounds like we're fucked then."

"So you believe me?"

"No, not at all. It's obvious to me that you've lost your mind. What's fucked is your relationship with Klyber. We can't allow someone in your state of mind to continue working here."

"I know my numbers have dropped lately, but it's hard to concentrate when I'm receiving all these notes. Would you like to see the rest of them? I have several."

His curiosity betrayed him, and he said, "Okay, show me the notes."

I took the notes from my pocket and tossed them onto the desk between us, all of them loosely folded together, and watched him read through them. After a minute he said, "This is meaningless drivel. Verbal excrement that could have been written by anybody." He tossed me the papers again.

"That's the exact same line of dialogue that Scott used earlier. He's recycling lines now," I said, stunned. "That can't be good."

"To be frank, none of this is good, Dan. Here's the deal. I am not a doctor of any kind, but it's obvious to me and some of you colleagues that at some point over the last few days or so you've gone crazy and are passionate about the ludicrous idea that you are the protagonist of a novel—"

"—Short story, actually. One of the things he told me just now in the bathroom was that it's no longer a novel, it's a short story. He's struggling, I presume."

"We're all struggling, Dan. Life is a struggle. I'm

struggling right now to tell you that I've arranged for you to speak with the Klyber psychologist, Dr. Petunia, about all of this. He is going to evaluate you and we will decide how to proceed after that."

"Mr. Lemming, please let me just say that I am fine. Aside from these notes, everything seems as normal as it ever has."

"Regardless," said Lemming with a wave of his hand, "I've already made the arrangements with the psychologist. He's waiting for you. I suppose you at least know where his office is located?"

"I do." I felt deflated. Kennard was sucking the air out of me line by line.

"Okay. You are expected to go to his office right now."

"Right now?"

"Yes. I'm going to call him and tell him you are on your way."

"But Mr. Lemming, I have plenty to do back at my—"

"—No buts, Dan. It's a done deal." On the phone, he poked a couple numbers and the psychologist answered right away. Lemming said, "Dan is on his way right now. Please let me know if he doesn't make it down there in a timely fashion," and then he hung up and looked at me over his desk. "You heard it. He's waiting for you."

"Mr. Lemming," I pleaded. "We don't have time for this. The end is coming at any moment. We should be saying our farewells."

"Isn't that up to Kennard? If you're to be believed, isn't *he* the one in charge of all this?" He held up his arms at everything around us, at the whole world. "If he wanted us to all be saying goodbye to each other, he would do it, would he not?"

"I suppose you're right, Mr. Lemming."

"Right now, he wants you to go see the psychologist. He's a fine man, that Dr. Petunia. You'll be able to tell him everything."

In the doorway I turned back to look at him. "Goodbye," I said.

"Fare well, Kennard," and then he actually looked up from his desk at me. "I mean it."

As I approached Dr. Petunia's office, he was waiting for me with the door open, sitting behind his desk in a white shirt and flower-patterned tie.

"Hello there, Dan. Come on in. Take a seat. I've been expecting you."

I sat down across from him in a very comfortable leather chair and looked around. His office was brightly lit and there were imitation petunias in just about every space where there could be.

"Tell me what's going on," he said, his notebook open on his lap.

"Well...a few days ago, I began receiving notes from a man named Kennard."

"And where did you find these notes?"

"The first one was stuck to my coffee maker. After that, I found another one the next day on my bedside table, and then here at work on my computer monitor, and on the door to my apartment, and—"

"—Okay, and what is the gist of these notes?"

"The gist is that I'm the protagonist of a short story and you and everyone else are side characters."

"So the idea is that this is all a fiction?"

"Yes."

"Taken to it's extreme, even the words I'm speaking

right now are the products of his mind, would that be right?"

"I suppose that's right."

"Okay. Do you have these notes?"

"I do."

"May I see them?"

"Absolutely."

I took the notes out again and handed them across the desk to him. He lifted his glasses up to look at them and then handed them back to me.

"Well? I'm not making this up, doctor. I hope you can see that."

"This last one says, 'Here goes nothing!' What do you suppose that means?"

"I know exactly what it means. I spoke to Kennard in the bathroom just a little while ago. He wrote himself in to tell me that he'll be ending the story any moment now. That's what he means."

"Did he say how he would do it?"

"No. I requested a happy ending, but he said he can't make any promises."

"I see."

Dr. Petunia leaned back in his chair as if to consider the matter, staring up into the rows of petunias that filled the space between the top of his cabinets and the ceiling.

"I must say, Dan, that this is all very compelling stuff, and as a so-called side character, I am concerned for myself as well. In all my years, I've never encountered this sort of issue before, if we can even call it that."

"So you believe me?"

"I want to. I want to believe you, but while these notes are compelling, before I go any further, is it possible that someone is playing a joke on you?"

"I suppose it's possible, but I don't know who it would be. Why start now?"

"Can you remember anything about your life *before* you began receiving these notes?"

I sat back in my own chair, stunned by the question, but even more stunned by the fact that I recognized that I couldn't. It was as if my life only went back a few days. Dr. Petunia must have seen my face grow confused.

"For example," he added. "Can you tell me where you went to college? Or where you met your girlfriend or wife?"

I thought for a moment, but nothing came to me. It was as if I had been concussed. Come to think of it, I didn't even know what day of the week it was. Kennard wouldn't tell me.

"I can't remember," I admitted, embarrassed. "What about you though? Where did you go to college?"

He glanced up at the framed diploma on his wall and said, "That's easy. Sunset City University."

"When did you start working here at Klyber?" I pressed.

"Now that is a good question. It feels like it's been a long time. I'm quite old after all. Look at me. My beard is gray these days and I feel like I need coffee to stay awake most of the time." He paused to think about it. "Dan, I fear you've got me here. Now that you've mentioned it, I cannot remember when I started working here."

"Neither can I. Our memory only goes back to the beginning of the story and whatever little bits Kennard has supplied us with. Isn't this proof that I'm right?"

"It may only prove that my memory is bad."

"Well which is it? Can all of our collective memories be bad?"

Suddenly there was a knock on his office door and I got a sinking feeling in my gut. The knock itself seemed real enough, but I was suddenly questioning everything around me in a way I hadn't before, taking every implication of the situation to the extreme. If Kennard was to be believed, the sudden appearance of someone outside the door and the knock were all just sentences on a page somewhere. I began to think I could walk through walls if Kennard wanted me to.

"Who is it?" called Dr. Petunia. "Can't you see that I'm with a client?"

The person knocked again and Dr. Petunia rose from behind his desk to go open the door.

"I wouldn't do that, if I were you," I said.

"Why do you say that?"

"I don't know. Why do I say anything? It must be Kennard putting words in my mouth again."

Dr. Petunia hesitated briefly and then looked at me. "I feel like I have no choice. I *must* open this door right now."

"Suit yourself," I said hopelessly.

He turned the handle and pushed the door open slightly, just enough to stick his head out and see who it was. From the other side of the door, I heard Petunia say, "Yes, can I help you?" and then in the next moment he was being pushed aggressively backwards into the office again by another man with a beard, who I recognized right away looked a lot like me. I also happened to recognize his black shoes. It was Kennard writing himself in again, and he had Petunia gripped by his flower-patterned tie and was forcing him back into his chair. He kicked the door closed behind him with his foot and then it was just the three of us in there.

Petunia's face was red and angry from the struggle. "For God's sake," he huffed. "What do you think you're doing?"

"I'm putting an end to all this once and for all."

Petunia looked at me as if for an explanation.

"Dr. Petunia," I said. "This is Kennard. He's the author of this story."

"So it's true," said Petunia with a look of terror. "What are you going to do to me?"

"Same thing I've done to countless others before you, which is simply leave you here in this scene forever. You've served your role here well enough. However, there is a bit of good news, which is that I may need you again someday since you are a relatively new invention of mine. There could be more parts for you to play yet, Dr. Petunia."

Petunia seemed to brighten at the idea of being used again at some point. "Thank you," he said modestly.

Next thing I knew Kennard and I were standing outside Lemming's closed office door.

"Knock," he told me, and so I knocked.

A few moments later, Lemming opened the door and saw the two of us standing there like twins. "Dan? What are you doing back here again? Who's this?"

"I'm Kennard and I'm here to put an end to all this."

Lemming shuddered and tried to close the door on us, tried to save himself, but Kennard blasted it open with a sentence and sent Lemming backing up into his office again until he tripped and fell behind his desk. Kennard approached and loomed over him while I stood behind and watched.

"Watch this," he said to me. Then he turned back to Lemming. "Say 'Poof'" he commanded.

Lemming looked up at him. "What? Why?"

"Just say 'Poof'" repeated Kennard.

Lemming, uncertain of whether or not doing as he was told would be of any benefit to him, hesitated.

"Say it!" screamed Kennard.

"Fine, I'll say it. I'll say it." He looked around his office one last time and then he said, "Poof" before disappearing immediately into thin air, leaving the two of us standing there in an empty office.

"Where did he go?"

"It doesn't matter," said Kennard, leading us back out. "Let's go get the others. Pull the door shut behind you."

"Why?" I asked.

"Because after we leave there will be no more office either. I'm getting rid of everything I've ever created and starting over. Clean slate."

"What will there be instead?"

"At first, there will be nothing but bright white light."

"Like an empty page."

"You got it."

"Now what?" I asked him.

"Now we get rid of everyone else too."

During the space break, Kennard had gathered the rest of us back in the conference room again. I was sitting next to Kennard and Gary was on the other side of me while across the table were Scott, Nancy, and Diane, who were visibly panicked. It felt like we were all there to be executed.

"Well, what do you have to say for yourselves?" asked Kennard.

"I'd like to know who you are," said Scott. "You can't call a meeting if you don't work here."

"I'm Kennard," he said. "I'm the author of all this, and I can do whatever the hell I want to."

Scott's face reddened, unused to being talked to that way. He started to say something back, but Kennard silenced him, deleting his dialogue so that he could only sit there moving his lips soundlessly.

"What do you plan on doing?" asked Nancy.

"Hand me one of your cigarettes, Nancy," said Kennard. "Your purse is under the chair." He turned to me. "You want one too?"

"Sure," I said, no longer feeling any concern for my health since I was nothing more than a string of sentences anyway.

Nancy took the pack from her purse and slid her last two cigarettes across the table to us along with a book of matches. We lit up while the other four looked on in silence and dread. Scott was trying to write something down on a piece of paper for us to read, but finding it impossible to compose a word. From my vantage point, it appeared as if he was scribbling circles. Enraged, he took out his phone from his pocket presumably to call for help, but as he pushed the buttons he found that his phone was turning to goo in his hand. It had never been a real phone in the first place and now it had become obvious.

Between drags, Kennard said, "Scott, I'm going to do you first."

The rest of us turned our eyes to Scott to see how he would react. He tried to throw the goo phone at Kennard, but it stuck to his palm instead and try as he might with his other hand he couldn't get it off.

"Scott, next to your chair is a large hammer. Pick that up now."

We watched as he leaned down and picked up a large hammer and held it in his hands, the goo phone smushed around it. "Now, I'm going to have you go over to that window out there in the office and smash it out with the hammer, and then I want you to jump."

"But we're thirty-three floors up, Kennard," said Gary.

"Do you think I don't know that?"

"They aren't *real* floors, Gary. You must understand that by now," I said, taking a long drag on my own cigarette and feeling totally fearless.

"Gary," continued Kennard, "I want you to follow Scott and bring back the hammer after he knocks the window out and jumps. We might need it in here."

Nancy and Diane both looked at each other anxiously, and then looked at me as if I would be able to help them somehow. I only shrugged and smoked some more.

Meanwhile, Scott stood from his chair and made his way to the office window overlooking the city below and Gary followed him just like Kennard had ordered, both of them totally helpless to alter course.

"While they're doing that, Nancy and Diane are going to bring us some coffee. Do you want some coffee, Dan?"

"Sure," I said.

"Why is he getting special treatment?" said Nancy.

"Nancy, please. Let's just go get the coffee," said Diane.

"It's already done, you just need to pour us two cups and bring them in here."

The two of them rose from their seats and went to the break room across the hall while Scott began banging at the window with the hammer and Gary stood behind him watching, then Kennard turned to me, the two of us alone briefly.

"You've been a good sport, Dan."

"Thanks." I smoked some more.

"I think I know what I'm going to do with you after we're done here. I think you'll like it."

"Okay," I said meekly, afraid to press him on any further details, and then Nancy and Diane came back with the coffee and placed them down in front of us.

"Thanks you two, you may return to your seats."

Outside the conference room, Scott had finished clearing out the window and handed the hammer to Gary before stepping up into the empty sill, his hands gripping each side, his feet teetering on the edge, his jacket and hair blowing in the stiff breeze that was now flowing into the rest of the office.

"Okay," said Kennard, "on the count of three, Scott is going to jump from the window. Everyone ready? Count with me." He looked at Nancy and Diane especially and they nodded, knowing nothing else they could do. We counted together aloud, "1-2-3!" and sure enough we watched Scott jumped out of sight right on three, like he couldn't wait to do it.

Gary leaned out through the window, stricken, presumably to watch him fall, and then came back to the conference room and sat down again with the hammer on his lap.

"Well?" said Kennard. "That wasn't so bad, was it?"

"What did you see, Gary?" asked Diane.

"Nothing. Scott was gone as soon as he fell. It's pure white outside now. The city is gone."

"Nothingness," I said, snuffing my cigarette out on the desk in front of me.

"That leaves the rest of us to deal with," said Kennard.

"I think Gary should try to eat that hammer," I said.

"Stellar idea," said Kennard, "even though I gave it to you." He laughed. "Do it, Gary. Eat that hammer."

"I don't understand," he said.

"You can't eat a hammer," said Nancy in utter disbelief.

"Sure you can. Go on, Gary, eat it. I will make it taste

like your favorite food."

He lifted the hammer to his mouth and bit into it, and sure enough he was able to take a bite from it. His eyebrows went up in surprise and he said, "It tastes like the best hot wings I've ever eaten." He chewed and took another bite, more eagerly than the first time, while Kennard and I sipped our coffee and watched as he continued to eat the hammer.

"Diane, come over and sit on Gary's lap. You've both always had a thing for each other anyway, right?"

Gary was pleasantly surprised as Diane came over and sat down on his lap, smiling at him as he chewed on the hammer with his cow-like jaw.

"It's true," she blushed. There was still a bit of the hammer left to eat, and Gary offered some to Diane.

"It tastes like red velvet cake to me," she said, and she took another small bite. They shared the rest of the hammer together romantically until it was finally gone and they were left licking their fingers.

"Gary, I want you to carry Diane over to the window there and the two of you can jump out together."

"So we're all just jumping out of windows now?" said Nancy. "Some ending," she scoffed.

We each sipped some more from our coffees as Gary lifted Diane and carried her out of the conference room, watching as they struggled their way into the open window sill. Diane had her arms wrapped firmly around Gary's shoulders, and he was able to hold her up briefly before they fell forward through the window and out into the pure white background that had replaced the view of the city.

"Dan, give Nancy the rest of your coffee."

"Okay," I said, and pushed the half-empty mug towards her. She reached out and pulled it the rest of the way across the desk.

"Nancy, pour the rest of Dan's coffee over your head."

"Whatever," she said, lifting the mug and pouring it into her hair. As it rolled down from her head and dripped onto her shoulders and blouse, it left strings of white space all over her where she seemed to have dematerialized.

"We need more," said Kennard. "Dan go get the rest of the pot and bring it in here."

I jumped from my seat to get it from the conference room, and then handed it to Nancy.

"Pour the rest over your head," commanded Kennard, and she did. It soaked her hair and ran down the front of her face and onto her shoulders and chest, preventing her from screaming as it soaking her blouse, and the two of us watched as she disappeared from sight, her head and shoulders just an empty white space against the background of the conference room. The only thing left of her was her torso and arms, which hung limply over the sides of the seat so that she appeared to be dead.

"She's gone now. Dan, go take her to the window and drop her out of here."

I went around the table and lifted the remainder of her body from the seat and into my arms and headed towards the open window. I worried about the coffee getting on me and doing the same thing, but it didn't appear to have the same effects. I had to remind myself that it wasn't the coffee, that it was Kennard who was responsible for all of this, and he had saved me for last.

I tossed Nancy's torso through the open window and leaned out to watch it fall, but like Gary had said earlier, there was nothing to see outside but pure white. I like to think that perhaps all of them are still together somewhere on the other side of whatever this world is, but only Kennard really knows.

I went back into the conference room where Kennard was sitting quietly and finishing his own coffee.

"It's time to wrap this up," he said, and he drank the rest down in one long swallow. "I'm afraid this will be goodbye for us, Dan. Thanks for being a good sport all these years."

I didn't know what he meant by that, being unable to remember anything beyond the last few days, but I was at least glad that he didn't make me jump out of the window like everyone else.

He let me live on a little longer.

Next thing I knew, I was standing in front of my apartment door again, and there was a note taped to it from Kennard. It said, "This ending will have to suffice for now, until I can come back and create a better one."

I snatched the note from the apartment door and put it into my pocket, then I went inside to find Layla reading something at the kitchen table, relieved to see that he hadn't gotten rid of her yet. She turned to me and smiled when she heard the door open.

"I've poured you a drink," she said.

I put my workbag down on the sofa and went and sat down across from her.

"What are you reading?" I asked.

"It's an article about a husband and wife, and the wife is sick with a terminal illness so they both decided to become cryonically frozen until a cure is found. Isn't that romantic?"

"It sure is," I said, taking a long drink of the scotch.

"Would you do that for me?"

"We both know that isn't up to me, babe, but I'd like to think I would. For now, though," I went on, smiling, "we'll just have to wait for Kennard to decide what he wants to do with us. Look." I showed her that last note. "He's going to come back one day and fix it for us."

"Unless he forgets about us."

"Do you think he would?"

"He could get involved with other projects, right? Start running with a bunch of new people?"

"I suppose so," I said. "But if he forgets about us, then what?"

"Then I guess it will stay like this forever."

"Forever," I echoed, and then I finished off my drink with one big gulp just before everything went poof.

Kennardo's Balloons

One day, as suddenly as he materialized into our world, he just as quickly went out of it again, like a candle blown out. But because so many people encountered him that day, once the stories stopped coming in the rest of us who hadn't seen him maintained an anxious hope that he would someday return. We wanted to hear more stories, while everyone who already encountered him wanted to encounter him again so they could hold up a fresh experience against their memories. He was like a drug for people, but it soon became apparent that the moment had passed and soon after that a nostalgic feeling was in the air for days gone by, when the possibility of encountering the clown still existed. The idea that there would be no new encounters with him, that there would be no new stories to tell, seemed impossible to accept.

I remember all of this very well because I was part of a group of graduate students at the time and it was my last semester in the Physics program. Professor Canard, a specialist and leading researcher in the field of Balloon Studies, heard about some balloons the clown was said to have made on the day he appeared, and so he put out notice requesting that anyone who had received a balloon animal from the man now known as Kennardo the Clown to please turn it in for a cash reward. As part of our grade he made us post signs all over the city, so we did. We embraced it with such idealism and hope because of the way he talked about it with us, and we admired the way he described it as a quest for Truth. Back then the search for a real Kennardo balloon felt like serious business. We went around stapling posters to light poles and taping them into local shop windows, we even took out an ad in the Sunset City Chronicle. Looking back, you could make the argument that our initial enthusiasm was just another cruel layer to it all.

It didn't take long for us to sense deep-down how it would all end because as we got to know him better it became clear he didn't understand what he was asking of people. The idea that things could have any emotional meaning beyond their measurable, material value had become foreign to him, evidence of mental weakness. He expected that by offering people a small sum of money for their Kennardo's, they would begin flooding in. He actually thought he would have to turn people away. Because he regarded Kennardo as a kind of visiting god to our universe, it was of utmost importance that we gather every artifact we could that he had left behind. Soon enough we joked behind his back that he was trying to extrapolate god from a bunch of balloons, and we made fun of him for expecting any children to show up once word got around. The problem was that he assumed everyone else thought the same way he did, but they didn't. Of course they didn't, and in the end not one child came. Seeing what happened to him after that, after all the jokes, we began to feel bad for him in a way. He was someone who revealed all the dark corners that came with living a complete Life of the Mind, so consumed by Elasticity Theory and Golden Inflation Ratios that he couldn't understand other people anymore.

Desperate to obtain a Kennardo, a week later he called a graduate student meeting to show us the promotional video he came up with and to ask us our opinions. He stood at the back of the room near the light switch and said in a booming, serious voice, "Ladies and gentlemen of the Physics program, particularly those of you in my Balloon Studies class, I expect you, of all people, being like-minded and what not, to understand why this is such important business not just for me, but for all of us together, and for the future of what it means to exist as people. For us, in our field of study, obtaining a Kennardo balloon is of utmost importance. Figures like a Kennardo pass through the world once an age, and we are lucky to have shared our time with him." He coughed hard into his shoulder and cleared his throat. "Primitive cultures, cultures of the past, etcetera, didn't know what they had before them, but we do. We sense the possibilities of further attention, and we shall do whatever we can to preserve our experience for future ages. Thank you." Then he turned the lights off and it started.

In the video, he was sitting behind the desk in his office looking eccentric and desperate. His eyes were a little too wide open and the lighting was poor, and he spoke a little too quickly for most people to follow, especially any child who might somehow come across the video. He occasionally slammed a fist onto the desk as a reflection of his passion. He appealed to the strong sense of duty he felt we should all share towards contributing to the advancement of knowledge, and he particularly addressed the children of Sunset City. To them, he framed it as an opportunity to make a mature decision and join the cause, and he forgave the children their ignorance for maybe not being old enough just yet to realize what an authentic Kennardo balloon would mean to someone like him and the ongoing quest for Truth. He went on to describe the nature of balloons in explicit detail, emphasizing their finite existence as something of scientific value, explaining the process of Deflation with the passion of someone who had been pitted against it his whole life. With the help of an animation student, he created 3-D visual aids within the video and animated models showing how molecules of air escape from even the soundest of balloons in hopes that the children and teenagers he relied on would understand the need to act right away, before it was all too late. It was clear that for Canard the act of Deflation represented the passing of time in the same way a clock does for most other people, and you could hear the urgency in his voice and see the desperation in his eyes by the end of it. He concluded the video by revealing that he was now offering double the original payout, a hefty sum indeed, enough to make me wish I had my own Kennardo balloon to give him.

When it was over he flipped the lights on again. "Thoughts?" he asked.

All anyone could do was sit on their hands and fidget in awkward silence, and then I raised my hand and said something I wish I never had. I should have stayed silent like everyone else, I should have stayed out of it. I felt the whole room turn towards me at once.

"Yes, Dan?"

"I think I speak for everyone in this room when I say, I think it will work this time."

Someone off to the side stifled a giggle but Canard heard him and cast a quick side-glance in his direction, then he looked back to me and said, "I appreciate that, Dan, and I truly hope you're not being sarcastic about all of this."

"Not at all, sir. We're rooting for you," I said, doubling-down in the moment.

"Thank you. If there are no other comments right now, feel free to send me an email if something comes to mind, and I believe you all have my address. I'll be posting the video later this week upon approval from the Administration. I also hope to air it on local television, so please do your part to share, and thank you all for coming," he said, and then we shuffled out, dismissed. No one stopped him. No one sent him emails warning him against his potential embarrassment. No one had the courage to tell him what we all felt deep down, and so a week later the video was posted and the commercials began airing during Saturday morning cartoons. As part of our grade, he told us to go around to all of the posters we put up around town and cross out the original reward and write in the new one, so we did. At the same time, Canard had taken to sleeping in his office every night so that he would always be available should anyone appear offering a balloon.

The story goes that one day he woke up to the sight of a group of teenage boys, standing outside the Physics building. They were huddled close together in their winter coats and gloves, their breath visible in the cold, their colorful balloon animals a bright contrast against the gray sky and dark colors of their winter clothing. From his vantage point out the second-floor office window, everything was shadowy and gray except for the vivid slashing colors of the balloons they held. He knew the opportunity to study a Kennardo balloon would be the pinnacle of his life's work, so he threw on his winter coat and knitted hat and ventured outside to greet the boys.

"Good morning, boys, I'm Professor Canard. I'm glad you've decided to help." The tip of his nose was already rosy from the cold, made brighter by the fact that the rest of his face was so pale. "What have we got here?" He rubbed his hands together and leaned towards the balloons to inspect them closer. Canard eyed the group of boys, their winter scarves fluttering in a gust of cold wind. "What are they supposed to be?"

"They're ducks," one of them said.

"Ducks, huh? I didn't know Kennardo made balloon ducks."

"Of course he does—that's all he ever makes," another one snarked.

The other boys grumbled their support, but Canard raised his eyebrows sharply.

"Is that right?" He paced in front of them slowly, pausing to look at each one's balloons, inspecting them like a sergeant. "These appear awfully inflated for being Kennardos," he said, reaching out and squeezing a red balloon duck between thumb and forefinger. "Kennardo was making balloons— what—almost a year ago now?"

Behind him, one of the boys punched another one of the boys in the arm, striking sharp and fast, and if I knew Canard at all, he no doubt perceived it as a subtle acknowledgement that the boys were lying, and further aggravated by their lack of knowledge regarding the process of Deflation, especially after the extensive video explanation he provided. If they had bothered to understand the video, they would know their ploy to turn in false balloons would never work without at least some attention to detail. He was tempted to explain it to them again right there on the spot, but instead he said:

"Did you boys think for one minute that I would be fooled by these balloons? Did you think I wouldn't notice that these are brand new and over-inflated? Do you think I can't tell the difference between a Kennardo and something from the party store?"

He snatched the red balloon duck from the boy in front of him and ripped it apart, twisting it until every part of it had popped, and then he bent down into the boy's face and asked him if he thought the Truth was something one can achieve through false means. When the boy said nothing, having not yet considered the question in his young life, Canard shouted into the boy's face and answered the question for himself.

"No! You can't!" He leaned back to address the rest of them. "Who put you up to this? Was it that damn clown?" he demanded. "You poison the quest for Truth and Understanding when you introduce Falsity, do you boys understand that? You must never allow something False to take the place of the Real. There is nothing more important for humanity than this idea. There is nothing more relevant to us all than the Truth!" As his rant went on, his face whitened and his nose and his cheeks glowed red in the cold from the effort, his eyes fierce with passionate idealism. "Did you know we're living through the downfall of mankind because of these tendencies? Probably not—you probably aren't even old enough to realize that yet. Some of you never will either, most of you will probably end up contributing to the problem by the looks of it. But don't worry, you'll be the ones living through the end, not me."

The boys were silent, unblinking, looking at him like he was crazy because by then he kind of was. By the time he came to the end, Canard had grown visibly weary, physically deflated, realizing in a flood that his frustration was wasted on the boys. They edged away from him towards the bicycles they had ridden in on.

"Go home," he said. "Go home, and take your other balloons with you." He stood in the gusting cold with his hands in his coat pockets, staring down at the bright red pieces of balloon scattered on the ground between them like an exploded heart, and he listened to them laughing as they rode away on their bikes.

The weeks continued to pass and still no one showed up with a balloon. It became hard not to feel sorry for him by that point. He sat forlornly in his office, growing thinner and paler, forced to question his own judgment, forced to consider the possibility that perhaps a true Kennardo doesn't actually Deflate, forced then to consider the idea that he may have destroyed and rejected the only Kennardos that would ever cross his path during his encounter with the boys. By the end of that semester, he was so bewildered by the lack of response that he allowed himself to wonder if Kennardo or the balloons had ever been real to begin with, or if he was enduring some kind of sustained psychosis. He told us this. He told anyone who would listen.

It seemed that once he allowed himself to think he may have lost his mind that was it, he could never recover from the thought of it. He was too baffled to ever clarify his thinking again, and the last day any of us saw him before he disappeared into retirement and we all went on with the rest of our lives, he called a meeting in his office. He told us that he imagined Kennardo laughing at him through those boys and that he had come to view his whole life as an elaborate prank—a cosmic joke set up from birth to always be chasing something he could never catch.

Made in the USA
Columbia, SC
23 November 2022

71638648R00133